MOMENT OF TRUTH

ADAM CROFT

BLACK CANNON
PUBLISHING

First published in Great Britain in 2022.

This edition published in 2022 by Black Cannon Publishing.

ISBN: 978-1-912599-78-3

A CIP catalogue record for this book is available from the British Library.

Printed and bound in Great Britain by Clays Ltd, Elcograf S.p.A.

MORE BOOKS BY ADAM CROFT

RUTLAND CRIME SERIES

1. What Lies Beneath
2. On Borrowed Time
3. In Cold Blood
4. Kiss of Death
5. Moment of Truth

KNIGHT & CULVERHOUSE CRIME THRILLERS

1. Too Close for Comfort
2. Guilty as Sin
3. Jack Be Nimble
4. Rough Justice
5. In Too Deep
6. In The Name of the Father
7. With A Vengeance
8. Dead & Buried
9. In Plain Sight
10. Snakes & Ladders

PSYCHOLOGICAL THRILLERS

- Her Last Tomorrow
- Only The Truth
- In Her Image
- Tell Me I'm Wrong
- The Perfect Lie
- Closer To You

KEMPSTON HARDWICK MYSTERIES

1. Exit Stage Left
2. The Westerlea House Mystery
3. Death Under the Sun
4. The Thirteenth Room
5. The Wrong Man

All titles are available to order from all good book shops.

Signed and personalised editions available at adamcroft.net.

Foreign language editions of some titles are available in French, German, Italian, Portuguese, Dutch and Korean. These are available online and in book shops in their native countries.

EBOOK-ONLY SHORT STORIES

- Gone

- The Harder They Fall
- Love You To Death
- The Defender
- Thick as Thieves

To find out more, visit adamcroft.net.

EXCLUSIVE MEMBERSHIP BENEFITS

Are you an avid reader of my books? If so, you can gain access to exclusive members-only books, content and more.

By subscribing to VIP Premium, you'll get a whole host of benefits and additional perks — and supporting me and my work directly.

Here are just a few of the benefits you can enjoy:

- **Up to 30% off** all online shop orders from adamcroft.net
- **Early access to new books** — up to *2 weeks* before release
- A **free ebook** of your choice
- **Free short stories**, not available anywhere else
- Have a **character named after you** in future books

- Access to **exclusive** videos and behind-the-scenes content
- A **personalised video message** from me
- Unlimited **free UK postage** (and reduced international shipping)
- **Your name in the Acknowledgements** of every new book
- Access to **exclusive** blog posts

To find out more, or to join today, head to **adamcroft. net/membership.**

HAVE YOU LISTENED TO THE RUTLAND AUDIOBOOKS?

The Rutland crime series is now available in audiobook format, narrated by Leicester-born **Andy Nyman** (Peaky Blinders, Unforgotten, Star Wars) and **Mathew Horne** (Gavin & Stacey, The Catherine Tate Show, Horne & Corden).

The series is available from all good audiobook retailers and libraries now, published by W.F. Howes on their QUEST and Clipper imprints.

W.F. Howes are one of the world's largest audiobook publishers and have been based in Leicestershire since their inception.

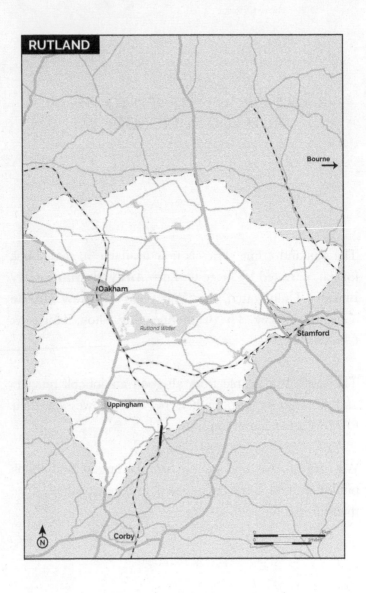

OAKHAM

Ashwell Road

Burley Road

Rutland Police

Oakham
Station

Cold Overton Road

West Road

High Street

Stamford Road

Uppingham Road

N

0   0   1km

0   1mile

For me this time.

1

Felicia Cooke was used to unlocking other people's doors, but this was the first time she'd ever been tasked with letting herself into a castle.

She willed her frozen fingers to turn the key more quickly, keen to get inside and away from the biting December chill. It had been a bitterly cold day, and the evening wasn't getting any warmer.

She felt glad they'd provided her with a key. 'Just in case,' they'd said. They'd assured her someone would be here to meet her, even though the castle had been closed to the public for over an hour. She wondered what she would have done without the 'just in case' key.

Grabbing a nearby chair, she propped the door open, allowing a little of the artificial light from outside to spill in, relieving some of the pitch darkness inside.

She fumbled her way through the castle and into the back rooms, desperately searching for a light switch and wishing she'd taken the time to find out how to use her phone as a torch.

Although Felicia was a relative latecomer to the events management industry, she felt she'd taken to it like a duck to water. It had proven tricky to get her business off the ground, especially in such a crowded market. Sometimes she wondered if she should have got on this particular bandwagon a little earlier. Then again, she hadn't anticipated it might involve groping her way around castles in search of light switches.

Eventually, she entered another room and found a switch on the wall next to the door. She flicked it on and off four times, but nothing happened. *Fuse must have blown*, she thought. Sighing, she took her phone from her pocket and Googled *iphone torch mode*. Moments later, she gave a small smile as the room lit up in front of her.

'Right,' she said to no-one but herself. 'Ah-ha.'

The fusebox sat boldly on the wall in front of her, as if having led her here itself. She strode over and lifted the cover, immediately spotting the master lever set to the 'off' position. She flicked it on, wincing as the lights sputtered into action overhead, bathing the room in an offensive glare.

She squinted and let herself back out of the room, keen to find a slightly darker area of the castle in which she could gradually allow her eyes to adjust to the light.

A few moments later, she found herself back in the main belly of the castle. She supposed it likely had a proper name. She doubted even the Normans would have called it a belly. In any case, Oakham Castle wasn't what she would have called a castle. It was more like a big hall, or a village church. She didn't suppose many invading armies would have been put off by the sight of it. Then again, the client was paying for the event, and the client wanted it to be held here.

She was aware of a little about the history of the castle — mostly that it had something to do with horseshoes — a fact she recalled as she found herself faced with an entire wall of them. Each one carried the name of a Lord or Duke of some sort, who'd presumably chosen to give an oversized horseshoe to the castle for whatever reason.

With her eyes now fully adjusted to the light, she turned and started to scout out the room, growing slightly annoyed that the space hadn't been cleared for her as promised. She'd have to have a word.

'Oh!' she squealed, feeling immediately embarrassed. 'Sorry, I didn't see you over there.'

The man didn't reply. She couldn't quite make it out from where she was, but he seemed to just be sitting, staring at her. She wished she'd brought her glasses.

'Are you the chap I'm meant to be meeting?' she asked, but got no response.

He was sitting in what appeared to be a judge's chair, high on a platform, behind a large desk with raised benches to either side of it, where she supposed a jury might sit.

First the locked door, then the power failure, not to

mention the time she was going to have to spend clearing away before she could get started. And now this rudeness.

She tutted and strode over to him, ready to give him a piece of her mind. But as she approached, the picture in front of her became ever clearer.

Her bold stride gradually slowed into a heavy saunter as her jaw began to fall.

'Oh my,' she said as she took in the scene.

The man hadn't been staring at her at all. And he certainly hadn't been ignoring her. Despite her confident exterior, Felicia Cooke was sure about very little in life. But there was now one thing about which she could be absolutely positive: this man was quite dead.

Dexter Antoine parked his car in the market square and walked up to the castle gate. By now it had been cordoned off, and he showed his identity badge to the officer who was guarding it.

'Let's designate this the outer cordon,' Dexter said, carrying out his first duty as bronze commander. 'Carry it on right round the edge of the castle grounds. Inner cordon on the castle itself.'

The officer nodded. 'Sarge. PCs Harding and Coulter are inside.'

'Lovely, thanks.'

Dexter walked across the car park towards the front door of the castle. It was the first time he'd visited in a work capacity, and it'd been a few years since he'd visited for leisure.

As he entered the castle, he greeted PC Ian Harding, who gave him a brief run-down of what they knew so far.

'We've got a male, late sixties, found sitting in the judge's chair with blunt force trauma to the skull. Discovered by that lady over there,' Harding said, nodding towards a woman in her forties who was being comforted by PC Coulter. 'She's an events organiser of some sort, and was coming in to set up. She said she arrived just before six, and the doors were locked so she had to let herself in. The power was off, so she stumbled around trying to put that back on, and then she came through to here, where she found the deceased in situ. She dialled the nines, but only requested ambo for some reason.'

'Oh?' Dexter asked, feeling his eyebrow rise. Under the circumstances, he would have expected someone uncovering this scene to have asked for the police, and not just an ambulance.

'Shock, apparently. She didn't know what to do.'

'Any idea what happened?'

'Not as yet. I did notice some evidence of marks on the top of the deceased's wrists, as if there'd been a struggle of some sort, but not much of one.'

'Show me?'

PC Harding led Dexter over to the body. 'Here,' he said.

Dexter looked more closely at the marks. 'Almost as if his wrists had been tied to the arms of the chair. No sign of any rope or anything?'

'No, nothing that we've found.'

Dexter took in the scene around him. 'Do we know where that is?' he said, pointing to a space on the wall where a horseshoe had been. All that remained in its place was a hook and chain.

'No idea. Taken down for cleaning or restoration, maybe? Looks like it's been taken off properly. Doesn't seem like the chain's snapped or anything. Plus we didn't find anything near the body, which I'd expect if it'd fallen down and killed him.'

'I'd also expect to find one dent in his skull rather than several, and for him to have probably not untied his arms and hidden the rope before coming back to finish dying.'

'Good point,' Harding replied, chastened, as Dexter took out his phone and snapped a photograph of the gap on the wall.

The officer who'd been manning the outer cordon stepped into the room. 'Sarge, you got a minute?'

Dexter followed him.

'The manager of the castle is here. Man by the name of Rupert Allard.'

'Ah, just the man I wanted to see,' Dexter called, before introducing himself to Allard. 'Probably best if we stay out here for the time being. Just while we wait for forensics.'

'What's happened? The woman on the phone said something about a body.'

'That's correct. We're still trying to ascertain what's happened. What time did the castle close today?'

'Four o'clock, same as always.'

Dexter did the mental maths. That meant there'd been

less than two hours between the castle closing to the public and the body being discovered.

'And who was in charge of closing, do you know?'

'That'd be Clive. Clive Thornton. He does Mondays.'

'Okay. What does Clive look like? Age, that sort of thing.'

'Uh, past retirement age, but not by much. Sixty-seven or sixty-eight, perhaps? I think he retired early. Probably about six feet tall, dark hair fighting the losing battle against grey, clean shaven. I've probably got a photo on here, as it happens,' Allard said. 'The council were thinking of giving the castle website a bit of a makeover and wanted photos of the volunteers, so I've been popping in every now and again to take some. Ah yes, here we go,' he added, handing his phone to Dexter. 'That's Clive.'

Dexter pursed his lips and handed the phone back to Allard.

'Is there anywhere we might be able to go and have a sit down?' he said.

3

Dexter and Rupert Allard watched as Clive Thornton's bagged body was removed from the castle and loaded carefully into the waiting vehicle.

'It's just all so surreal,' Allard said as he unlocked the door to the Castle Cottage Café, recently relocated to the castle grounds itself.

'At least it'll be a little warmer in here,' Dexter replied, pleased that the café was locked off separately from the rest of the castle. At least this way he could argue it being outside of the inner cordon. 'I hope you don't mind, but I do need to ask you a few routine questions,' he added, taking a seat opposite Allard at one of the café's tables.

'No, I understand,' Allard replied. 'I suppose you want to know where I was earlier on, and whether anyone was with me.'

Dexter smiled. 'That'd be a good start. Sorry to have to ask, especially at a time like this.'

'It's fine, don't worry. I had a meeting with the council at five-thirty, which lasted just over an hour. Before that, I left home at about ten past five, and went straight there. My wife was at home with me.'

'And where's home?'

'Cottesmore.'

Dexter nodded as he wrote this down in his notebook. He'd need to verify Allard's account, but on the face of it he seemed to be out of the picture.

'There is something else I wanted to ask you,' Dexter said, changing the subject. 'The horseshoes on the wall in the Great Hall. Are they all meant to be there?'

'Yes, of course,' Allard replied, looking a little confused. 'No-one quite knows why, other than it being a tradition that goes back well over five hundred years. We've got over two-hundred-and-thirty of them, all donated by Peers of the Realm who've visited Rutland or passed through it. The oldest one was given by King Edward IV in 1470.'

'Very impressive,' Dexter replied. 'What I meant was whether the complete collection was on the wall or if any had been taken down for cleaning or restoration. Only I noticed one was missing, from right above the chair where Clive's body was found.'

'Oh. Well no, not that I know of. And I would know, I hope.'

'I took a photo, if that helps. Maybe it might ring a bell.'

Dexter took his phone out of his pocket, opened the photo and showed it to Rupert Allard.

'Oh my,' Allard replied. 'Yes, I know exactly which one was there.'

'Go on.'

'That was from Princess Margaret, Queen Elizabeth the Second's sister. It sits right next to The Queen's horseshoe from 1967. Her Majesty presented hers to the castle herself. She came on the Royal Train and walked from Oakham Station up to the castle. It's technically a racing plate, with the actual horseshoe of one of her favourite racehorses in the centre. Aureole, the horse was called. Finished second in the Derby on the year she was crowned. Princess Margaret's horseshoe was a white one. Smaller, in the traditional shape.'

'And there's no reason you can think of as to why that horseshoe would have been removed?'

'Absolutely not,' Allard replied. 'It makes no sense at all.'

'What about some sort of symbolism?' Dexter asked.

Allard furrowed his brow and rubbed his chin. 'Of that particular horseshoe? I don't know. I mean, it's the Queen's sister. Surely that's highly significant in itself. But as for the horseshoes generally… Well, there's got to be a reason, hasn't there?'

'Has there?' Dexter asked.

'Well, yes. I presume that's why you're asking. I mean, it's quite an elaborate amount of effort for someone to have gone to, isn't it? Somehow getting into the castle after closing time without being seen, having brought tools to unfasten and remove the horseshoe from the wall, then having to somehow dispose of a whopping great horseshoe with Princess Margaret's name embossed on it... It makes no sense at all. Why not just whack him round the head with the tool in the first place?'

'They may well have done,' Dexter said, his suspicions raised. 'We're only presuming the horseshoe *was* the murder weapon. Without finding it, we have no way of knowing, but the post-mortem will certainly tell us a lot more.'

'Let's hope so,' Allard said, seemingly placated and not registering Dexter's suspicion. As Allard continued, he leaned in towards Dexter, almost conspiratorially. 'If you ask me, there might be some sort of symbolism in the horseshoes themselves.'

'Oh?'

'The history is quite interesting, actually. You probably already know the horseshoe is a symbol of luck. It's steeped in superstition. Now, have you noticed that the horseshoes in the Great Hall are all hanging upside down? One would usually expect to see them presented with the toe at the bottom and the heels and quarters at the top, making a sort of "U" shape. But in Rutland, horseshoes are always displayed upside down. Even on the county's coat of arms.'

'Why?' Dexter asked, feeling himself being drawn in through intrigue.

'A couple of reasons. Some people believe having the

heels at the top represents the two horns of the devil. There's another theory that displaying the horseshoes upside down stops the devil from being able to make a nest in them. I think you have to be a certain type of person to believe in any of that, though. Personally, my favourite explanation is much nicer. With the horseshoes being so symbolic of luck, there's a theory that hanging them upside down means the luck falls out on whoever happens to be underneath one.'

Dexter lifted his eyebrows and sighed. 'Yeah, well I'm not sure Clive Thornton would agree with you on that one.'

4

Caroline felt a familiar warmth inside her as the sound of the turboprop plane receded into the distance. But underneath that tranquility was a deep sense of unease.

As the noise of the aircraft faded, she once again noticed the water lashing itself against the rocks, seeming to increase in volume all the time. She'd often found herself looking up at planes passing overhead, wondering who was on board and where they were going. She sometimes wished she could go with them.

She looked over at Harry, sitting on the riverbank, a lock of his golden hair releasing itself from its mooring behind his ear, before dangling softly in front of his eyes, waiting, daring to be tucked back into place. She couldn't see what book he was reading, but it looked big. A 'hefty tome', her father would have said.

She called out to him, wondering if he'd seen her. She got no response. Fearing he hadn't heard her over the sound of the frothing stream, she called again, louder this time.

Harry slowly lifted his gaze to look up at her. Even from this distance she could see his eyes. The blue was iridescent. Searing, almost. Before Caroline had properly taken it in, Harry lowered his head with the same smooth action as he'd lifted it.

Caroline narrowed her eyes. Had he blanked her? At least before she could convince herself he just hadn't heard her, but now she was left in no doubt.

As she stepped forward to go over and speak to him, she heard a yelp coming from the direction of the river. She looked across and saw her brother, Stuart, the rushing water throwing him against the rocks as he fought to keep his head above the surface.

Her legs felt heavy, as if made of lead, as she staggered her way over to the edge of the stream. Before she could make up her mind whether it was safer to jump in or stay there, she noticed the flow of water bringing Stuart closer to her. He seemed to be out of the worst of it, but he wouldn't be safe until he'd reached the water's edge.

Caroline glanced back over her shoulder towards Harry, who was still engrossed in his book, seemingly oblivious to the scene unfurling in front of him.

'Harry! Help!' she yelled, sure that her voice had carried this time.

Harry looked up once again, the bright summer sunlight shining onto his face. Again, the first thing she noticed was his eyes. But this time they looked different.

The blue had gone, replaced by a deep red, almost black. Before she could reason it, Harry lowered his head once more.

Caroline turned back to Stuart, who was clambering through the calmer waters, having almost reached the edge. She could see the lacerations to his shoulders and the blood running down the side of his head.

'Stu, hold onto my hand!' she called, reaching out her arm as far as she safely could.

A few moments later, Stuart reached her.

'Come on. Hold onto me,' Caroline said. But Stuart stayed still, simply looking at her.

She hadn't noticed the silence. It hadn't occurred to her that the water had become completely still, as if the river had stopped flowing. The only thing that made her realise was the rumbling that she now heard building in the distance.

As she looked upstream, she saw the frothing wave, growing as it came towards them, towering overhead.

By now, the rumbling had become a colossal roar, but through it she heard Stuart's soft voice as clear as day.

'Come with me,' he said, as he took hold of her hand with a vice-like grip. 'It's time.'

Before she could respond, Stuart hurled her into the river with a strength she could never have imagined, as the pressure of the water and the weight of the darkness came crashing down on top of her.

. . .

Caroline lurched as she gasped for breath. The heavy water had become a suffocating duvet, the frothing torrents a pool of cool sweat on her bedsheets.

She glanced over at her bedside table and reached for her phone, silencing the alarm. It wasn't a sound she was usually glad to hear first thing in the morning. But today, she decided, she'd allow it.

5

It was certainly a change of pace for Caroline, compared to what she was used to. It had been a few months since she'd decided to hand over more operational control of major incidents to Detective Sergeant Dexter Antoine, but this was the first time it had been put into practice in a big way.

She had absolute confidence in Dexter, and felt completely comfortable as he gave her a full run-down of what they knew so far. Even so, she had to keep reminding herself that her only responsibility now was to oversee investigations — not to run them.

Since Clive Thornton's death the previous evening, the cogs of the investigation — which the computer had named Operation Titan — had already begun to turn.

'His wife, Susan, was informed of her husband's death within the hour,' Dexter said, having laid out the basic information as to what they'd found at the scene. 'They covered the preliminary stuff for COPEGS, but we're intending to do a full in-depth meet with her this morning.'

COPEGS, yet another police acronym, was a helpful acrostic for updating the control room following a sudden death. It meant the officer would report back on the *circumstances* of death, *other* marks or suspicious circumstances, *position* of the body, *examination* by a doctor or paramedic, *general* health history of the deceased and the *sergeant's* review.

'Anything interesting come out of that?' Caroline asked.

'Nothing major,' Dexter replied. 'Although it was noted that Mrs Thornton's reaction seemed to be a little odd.'

'Odd? How so?'

'It might just be one of those situations where people respond differently. Impossible to say until we get to know her a little better, but apparently she completely broke down for a minute or so, then she seemed to pick herself up and get on with it all as if it was a normal everyday occurrence to find out your husband had just been murdered.'

'Weird,' Caroline replied. 'But yeah, that might just be her way of dealing with it. Who's going to see her?'

'I was going to pop down, either with Sara or Aidan.'

Caroline pursed her lips. After their last murder enquiry, the powers-that-be had promised her an extra permanent member of staff and access to quick deployment of additional temporary manpower if needed.

So far, this hadn't come to fruition, and was unlikely to do so within the next hour. Without that, they couldn't afford to lose either one of DCs Sarah Henshaw or Aidan Chilcott for the hours that would be needed to speak to Mrs Thornton in greater detail.

'I'll come with you,' she said, before adding, 'if you don't mind and it's alright with you, I mean. There's only so much paper I can push around here, and it'll mean you don't need to lose any bodies from the incident room.'

Dexter shrugged. 'Fine with me. Just you remember who's in charge, though, yeah?' he added, with his trademark cheeky smile.

Caroline let out an involuntary snort. 'I have a feeling you're not going to let me forget. What else do we know about Clive Thornton?'

'He and Susan had two kids, Ross and Emma, who both moved away for work after they'd finished uni. Ross lives in Italy, and Emma's down in Bristol. Clive was a retired businessman, mostly in the renewable energy industry from what I can decipher. If the house is anything to go by, he earned a fair bit of money. According to his wife, he did a lot of charity work and voluntary stuff, even before he'd retired, and that was something he'd carried on with.'

'Hence working at the castle.'

'Yup. His wife said he was the sort of person who needed to be doing something. He couldn't do sitting around and relaxing.'

Caroline smiled. 'I know the feeling. Any potential names cropped up at all?'

Dexter shook his head. 'Nope, afraid not. But that's the angle of attack we're going to have to start with, I think.'

'Nothing of any use at the scene that can lead us to someone?'

'Clean as a whistle. The murder weapon was nowhere to be seen. We've carried out an extensive search of the castle grounds and the surrounding area, but nothing. We're still waiting on post-mortem results, but the horseshoe looks like the most likely culprit.'

'What about CCTV?'

'Unfortunately not. The main electric fuse had been switched off. There was no power through the castle at all.'

'What about a battery backup?'

'Apparently not.'

Caroline let out a sigh. 'Why on earth do people go to all the effort of putting CCTV systems into these places and then choose one that can be defeated with the flick of a finger?'

'Search me,' Dexter replied. 'We took what there was in terms of footage, though. Just before the recording stops, you can see Clive locking the main door to the Great Hall, a few minutes after four. Pretty much as soon as he's done that and turned round, it cuts out.'

'And that was definitely because of the fuse tripping?'

'We reckon so. The error log on the CCTV system says the recording stopped due to a power failure.'

'Convenient timing, isn't it? The moment he locks the door to the public, the place is plunged into darkness.'

Dexter nodded slowly. 'Yup, pretty much. There would've been a bit of light, but not a lot. Sunset started at three-fifty and ended at half-past-four. Apparently.'

Caroline thought for a moment. 'So they couldn't have done it earlier, because the castle was open to the public. And they couldn't wait any longer... why? What time would Clive normally leave after closing up?'

'His wife expected him home not long after half past, so he wouldn't have hung around much longer.'

'So whoever killed him must have been familiar with his routine. They either knew him well, or had been watching him for a while. Was the wife at home on her own?'

Dexter nodded again. 'Yep. Mobile cell site triangulation backs that up, or at least shows that her phone was at home. She doesn't drive, and it would've been a huge risk for her to take public transport. We're checking the buses and taxi companies anyway, just in case. She called Clive's phone just before five o'clock, and she was at home then.'

'Any friendly neighbours happen to have CCTV?'

'Not that would show anyone leaving or arriving at the Thorntons' home, no.'

'And I'm guessing the Thorntons didn't have CCTV of their own?'

'Nope.'

'We can't rule her out just yet, then,' Caroline said.

'But it would've been one hell of a risky undertaking, considering the circumstances. There'd be much easier ways of doing it.'

'Unless that's what we're meant to believe.'

'Focus on finances. If Clive Thornton'd had a good business career and had a bit of money put away, it'd make him a target for all sorts. There might even be something business-related. Money can make people do some weird and wonderful things.'

'On it,' Dexter replied. 'Oh, and by the way, do we have any news on those extra reinforcements?'

Caroline gave a sympathetic eye-roll. 'What do you think? It's the usual story — all talk and promises, and no action. I'm going to request an urgent meeting with the Chief Super this morning. And this time I'm going to put my foot down.'

Dexter smiled and tried not to chuckle. 'Good luck.'

'Thanks. I have a feeling I'm going to need it.'

6

Caroline parked her Volvo on the impressive semi-circular driveway that swept past Clive and Susan Thornton's house.

'Horseshoe-shaped driveway,' Dexter quipped. 'He should've seen the signs.'

Caroline tried to stifle a laugh. Gallows humour was notorious for helping police officers get through some of the most difficult aspects of the job, but there was a time and a place. Seconds before meeting a distraught widow, and on her driveway, was not a good combination.

'Stop it,' she said, opening her door and climbing out. 'Best face please, Detective Sergeant.'

'This one's the best I've got, I'm afraid.'

Caroline let out a mock sigh. 'Well, I suppose the woman's already at rock bottom, so I doubt things could get any worse for her.'

Before they'd reached the front door, they heard the

sound of it being unlocked. They watched as the door opened, a man in his early forties waiting to greet them. He extended his hand as they approached.

'Hi, I'm Ross,' he said. 'Clive's son.'

'Hi, Ross. I'm Detective Inspector Caroline Hills and this is my colleague, Detective Sergeant Dexter Antoine.' Caroline looked at Dexter, whose slightly raised eyebrow told her all she needed to know. 'DS Antoine is running the investigation into your father's death,' she continued, 'so I'll let him lead the conversation today.'

'That's fine. Come on through,' Ross replied, walking back into the house as Caroline and Dexter followed him. 'Apologies if I'm not quite with it this morning. I've only been back in the country a couple of hours.'

'You did well to get a flight at such short notice,' Caroline said.

Ross shrugged. 'No other option really, is there? You drop everything and run.'

They arrived in the Thorntons' impressive kitchen, where Ross introduced Caroline and Dexter to a woman of a similar age to him, but who'd clearly been making efforts to look younger.

'This is my sister, Emma,' he said.

'Pleased to meet you,' Caroline replied, introducing herself. 'You live in Bristol, is that right?'

'Yes,' Emma replied.

'Did you come back this morning too?'

'No, last night when Mum called. 'I wanted to get back as soon as possible so Mum didn't have to spend the night on her own. Not that any of us got much kip anyway.'

'I can only imagine,' Caroline said, sympathising with the sea of red eyes in front of her, the scars of hours of agonised crying and very little sleep. 'It must have come as quite a shock.'

'It's the way he went that upsets me most,' Ross replied. 'I mean, you sort of expect and know your parents will go one day. You brace yourself for that. But not like this.'

Caroline looked at Susan Thornton, who had barely taken her eyes off the cup of tea in front of her. The dark film on the surface and the lack of steam told Caroline it had been some time since it was warm.

'Can I make anyone a cup of tea or coffee?' she asked.

'I'll do it,' Emma said, standing.

'No, it's okay. I can take care of it, and you can focus on speaking with my colleague. It'll give me something to do, and stop me butting in.'

Dexter gave a thankful but knowing smile.

'Firstly,' he began, 'I just wanted to say how sorry I am to hear what happened to your father. We'll leave no stone unturned in finding the person who did this. I know you'll want justice for him, and for yourselves, but I also appreciate that won't come close to repairing or helping the way you feel. The thing we hear most often from bereaved families is that justice and answers allow them to turn a page and begin the next chapter. It's a form of closure, as much as I don't like the word.'

'That feels such a long way from where we are now,' Emma said. 'Everything's just so... It doesn't seem real. I can't even describe it. It's like time has stopped, but only in this house. Everything else is still carrying on as normal. I came downstairs this morning after I finally gave up on sleep, and put the telly on. It was the news channel Dad always used to watch. And I sat there and I watched it. And the weirdest and most upsetting thing was that everything was still going on as it always has. Wars, the NHS crisis, even the bloody football results. And my immediate reaction was *Why the hell are they still playing football?* It sounds crazy now I say it, but it just feels so cold that the rest of the world is still turning, when ours has stopped.'

'I know what you mean,' Ross added. 'It was the same at the airport. People coming back from holidays, jetting off for Christmas, carrying on with their lives. It seemed so weird.'

Dexter gave a sympathetic smile. 'It's something we hear a lot. And lots of things will seem strange for a while. I know it might not feel like it at the moment, but it will get better. Time's a great healer, even if you might want to slap me for saying it now. But the best thing we can do for you is to find out who did this, and to get justice for you all.'

Ross and Emma nodded, while Susan continued to stare into her cup of cold tea.

'I know the instinctive answer might be "no", but can you think of anyone who might have wanted to cause harm to your father?' Dexter asked. 'It could be something recent, or much further back. Even if it might seem small and insignificant to you, you'd be surprised what some people consider to be big enough to make them do something like this.'

'That's just the thing,' Ross replied. 'There really isn't anything, or anyone. I know I don't see my parents much anymore because I live in Italy, but I know Dad. He'd never upset anyone. He spent his life giving all his spare time to charities and good causes. All he wanted to do was help people. That's what gave him pleasure. He just wasn't the sort of person to fall out with anyone.'

'The only thing I can think is that it was a case of mistaken identity,' Emma said. 'They must have got him mixed up with someone else.'

'It's a possibility,' Dexter said, being honest but not wanting to get their hopes up. 'We always consider everything. But either way, we need to make sure justice is done.'

Caroline brought the tea and coffee back to the table and sat down. 'It must give you some comfort to know that your dad was appreciated and loved by so many people,' she said.

Before either Ross or Emma could answer, Susan's chair flew back with a low squeal against the floor tiles, as she stood and walked purposefully towards the sink.

Caroline's first thought was that Susan was going to be sick, but she watched as the widow took the cleaning cloth that had been hanging over the tap, then pulled a bottle of surface spray from the cupboard below and began to wipe down the worktops with far more vigour than was necessary.

Caroline's eyes met Ross's, as they shared a sympathetic glance. He didn't seem overly surprised at his mother's reaction, but there was an undeniable element of concern.

'Leave that for now, Mum,' Emma said. 'We can do that later. Come and sit back down.'

'It's fine,' Susan said, her first words since Caroline and Dexter had arrived. 'It needs doing. I can still hear.'

Over her years in the job, Caroline was certain she'd seen every possible way of dealing with shock and grief. Some people collapsed into a heap, whereas others pushed everything down and strode on in denial. She was yet to be convinced any one approach was better than another, but observing them gave her an insightful glimpse into the sort of person they were, and how their minds dealt with tricky situations.

Dexter continued to steer the conversation and find out more about Clive Thornton. Caroline felt thankful she could take a back seat, as she watched the reactions and body language of the three people in front of her with growing interest and intrigue.

7

Caroline and Dexter arrived back at the police station following their chat with Susan Thornton, both their stomachs rumbling in anticipation of a long-overdue lunch.

'I'll be in in a sec,' Dexter said, noticing the time as they reached the front entrance. 'Just got to make a quick phone call.'

He waited until Caroline was inside, then walked a little further away from the building and paced through the car park as he scrolled through his phone. He knew a simple text message wouldn't cut it. In any case, he wanted to speak to her. Needed to. Hearing her tone of voice would be crucial. He knew from years of experience how she managed to hide things and put on a brave face, but he was sure by now he'd be able to see through it.

Considering this for a moment, he switched to WhatsApp, scrolled down until he found the conversation with her, opened it up and then pressed the icon for a video call.

He held the phone in front of him and watched the screen as the phone rang. A few moments later, the call connected, and Dexter saw a quick flash of blue sky before the screen went dark and the sound became muffled.

'Hello?' came the voice from the other end.

'Mum, it's me. It's a video call, so you need to take the phone away from your face.'

'Oh, my word. You're very loud, Dexter. Can you speak quieter?'

'It'll be on speakerphone. It's a video call. You're not meant to have the phone next to your ear.'

'Then how else am I going to hear you?'

'Hold the phone in front of you, Mum. Like a camera.'

'Like this?'

'The other way round,' Dexter replied, seeing only grass and a pond. 'Turn it round so you can see the screen.'

A moment later, his mum's face flashed into view. 'Oh, blimey. You gave me a fright, Dexter. What are you doing?'

'It's a video call, Mum. I wanted to see you as well as speak to you.'

'Well you could have said. You frightened me half to death. What's the matter?'

'I was just phoning to see how you got on.'

'Oh, fine, fine,' she replied. Although Dexter couldn't see, he knew she'd be doing her customary dismissive hand wave just out of shot. 'I'm just having a little sit down in the park while your father gets some coffee from the kiosk. Thought we'd make the most of the sunshine while we're out.'

'What did they say?'

'Who?'

'The hospital, Mum.'

'Oh, not a whole lot. You know what these doctors are like.'

In that moment, Dexter knew the doctor had almost certainly said quite a lot, and he could tell she hadn't liked it. In normal times, she held doctors almost in a state of reverence, it having been her life's ambition for Dexter to become one himself. For her to speak ill of one now could only mean one thing.

'Did they mention anything about the blood tests? What were the results?'

'They want to do some other tests now, apparently,' his mother replied, deftly dodging the question.

'Okay. Is that because of what the blood results said? Otherwise they would have done all those tests the last time, surely.'

'You'd think so. But the more often they can drag us in, the more money they'll get from the car parking charges.'

'I don't think that's their main motivation, Mum,' Dexter replied.

He watched as his mum's eyes darted up and to the side, as if she'd just spotted something — or someone.

'Okay, well I'd better get going,' she said. 'I'll speak to you later.'

'Is that Dad? Can I speak to him quickly?'

'Sorry, my love. My battery's really low. How do I end this call? Is it the—'

Dexter watched as his mum's face disappeared from the screen and the display switched back to their last WhatsApp chat. Whether she knew it or not, she'd told him everything without even needing to say a word.

8

As she and Dexter arrived back at the office, Caroline felt even more confused than she had previously. The initial conversations with a bereaved family tended to go one of two ways. They'd either reveal information that led them closer to identifying their killer, or they'd throw more spanners in the works and open up even more avenues of possibility than there'd been previously. When it came to Clive Thornton, though, they seemed to have moved no further in either direction.

However they looked at it, it made no sense. As a man of good standing and with an impressive record of charity and voluntary work, there seemed to be no reason why anyone should want him dead. The longer the conversation had gone on, the more Caroline had felt herself coming round to his daughter's suggestion that this had been a case of mistaken identity, and that Clive had simply been caught in the crossfire. But the more she thought about it, the less that made sense.

Clive Thornton's murder had been undeniably deliberate. Multiple head trauma was a pretty horrendous way to kill someone, and you had to want them dead. For Clive to have been led or dragged over to the judge's chair and restrained before he was beaten would've given ample opportunity for a case of mistaken identity to reveal itself. The only possibility Caroline could see was that the killer had been a hired hitman of some sort, and that Clive's protestations of innocence would have fallen on deaf ears. But even that theory had its drawbacks. Apart from the fact that the idea seemed a million miles away from Rutland, would a hired hitman have got things so wrong? And why would they have killed him in the way they did? Why not something easier, simpler, less symbolic? From Caroline's experience working in London, those sorts of hits tended to involve drive-by shootings, house fires and beatings in alleyways.

Whichever way Caroline looked at it, it made very little sense. It was a perfect example as to why detectives were trained not to come up with their own theories and design the search for evidence to fit them. Instead, the evidence must always be used to reveal the truth. Of course, each officer on a case would still have their own personal theories about what had happened. That was just human nature and psychology, and there'd be no stopping that. The key was not to let it cloud one's judgement or change the shape of an investigation.

She parked her thoughts to one side as she knocked on the door of Chief Superintendent Derek Arnold's office. She'd enjoyed a positive if unpredictable relationship with her superior officer since she'd arrived in Rutland, and had gradually formed the impression that Arnold was a spiritual ally. In practice, he could only be as helpful as the unseen forces above him, but over time he'd led Caroline to believe that he was at least on her side rather than theirs, and that he felt as hamstrung by budget cuts and unnecessary paperwork and procedure as she did.

As she sat down across the desk from him, she watched as he put his now-empty coffee mug back down and wiped his upper lip with his forefinger.

'So. Here we are again,' he said, with a wry smile. 'England's safest county. For now. Then again, being the smallest county does help somewhat. I don't think I'd like to see the murder rate per head of population over the last couple of years.'

'Nor me, sir,' Caroline replied. 'Although, from memory, I don't think we could have done much to prevent any of them, so we can only judge success based on our charge rate.'

Arnold raised an eyebrow and smiled. 'Very clever. I like your style. But listen, you know you don't need to justify anything to me. I've been pushing hard for extra resources for you. And I've already spoken to the powers-that-be and primed them about allocating additional support for Operation Titan. You let me know what you need, and we'll make sure you get it as quickly as possible.'

'Thank you,' Caroline said, feeling supported but not yet reassured. She'd spent enough years in the job to have experienced plenty of lip service and over-confident promises. 'That'll be very helpful. Invaluable, in fact. But we really do need that extra DC. Support staff are all well and good, but there's no replacement for a decent detective.'

'I know,' Arnold said, leaning back in his chair. 'And that's been a much tougher nut to crack. With national funding as it is, we're all being told we need to "find efficiency savings". That's politician talk for "get rid of people and make the others do more work". We're having to fight tooth and nail to keep officers and replace the ones who leave, never mind trying to justify increasing staff numbers. But we've got an iron in the fire.'

'Okay,' Caroline replied, becoming ever more confused. 'And can I ask what that is?'

'Let's just say our friends over at EMSOU aren't quite the rogues we make them out to be.'

EMSOU — the East Midlands Special Operations Unit — was the regional unit tasked with tackling serious and violent crimes on behalf of local forces. Under Caroline's leadership, Rutland had managed to wrest back local control over these cases — a situation that was heavily dependent on their continued success.

Caroline raised her eyebrows. 'You've managed to get someone to transfer over?'

'Mmmm. Secondment, technically,' Arnold said, cocking his head and avoiding her gaze. 'But that's just the foot in the door. We'll be looking to make it a permanent transfer. If all goes well, and if we can show we're not only in greater need but that the secondment is helping everybody, I see no reason why we won't be able to make it permanent.'

If only it were up to you, Caroline thought. 'Thank you,' she said. 'That'll be really useful. Do we have any idea of timescales?'

'Imminently,' Arnold said, with his characteristic talent of somehow managing to avoid committing to anything specific. 'I've already made them aware of Operation Titan, and fortunately for us they're going through a nice Q period at the moment. I know you've heard it all before, but I'm confident you will have an extra detective on this case very soon.'

Caroline nodded, aware that this was the closest thing she was going to get to an assurance. 'That's great to hear, sir,' she replied. 'You'll let me know when you hear more?'

'You'll be the first person I call. Keep your phone on you.'

Caroline left the Chief Superintendent's office feeling more reassured than she'd expected, confident that a new member of staff on the major incident team would make a huge difference to their chances of identifying and apprehending Clive Thornton's killer.

As she got back to her office, Aidan intercepted her.

'Sorry to bother you, ma'am, but DS Antoine's

stepped out for a moment. I just wondered, did Susan Thornton mention anything about a burglary? I don't recall anything from the notes.'

'Burglary? No, she didn't. What burglary?'

'At their home. It popped up on the PNC when I was running the routine checks. Clive and Susan Thornton were burgled three weeks ago.'

9

'Why on earth wouldn't they mention something like that?' Caroline asked of nobody in particular.

By now, Dexter had returned. 'She can't have told the kids,' he said. 'One of them would've brought it up. It might have nothing to do with what happened to Clive, but all that guff about having absolutely no idea where to begin? Surely being targeted by criminals only three weeks earlier would've been worth mentioning at that point.'

'What are the details?' Caroline asked Aidan.

'This is where it gets even weirder,' Aidan replied. 'Entry was forced through the back door, which was one of those old wooden ones. It happened sometime overnight, but they couldn't be any more specific because the first they knew about it was when they came downstairs the next morning and found the back door open and a pane of glass smashed.'

Dexter snorted. 'Imagine having a house so big that

you don't even hear someone kicking in your back door in the middle of the night.'

'The notes seem to indicate that the burglars must have been spooked by something, because there was no sign of anything having been taken. Officers didn't even attend — just the usual helpful email with tips on how to beef up their home security.'

'That obviously fell on deaf ears,' Caroline said. 'A place like that, and they don't even have a CCTV camera.'

'I think it reads very differently now, though,' Aidan replied. 'Especially in light of what happened to Clive Thornton last night.'

'What, you think breaking into his house could have been some sort of warning?' Dexter asked.

Aidan shrugged. 'Could be. They obviously weren't there for his TV and jewellery. Maybe they were after something else. Something bigger. Perhaps last night was a blackmail attempt gone wrong.'

'Who phoned the police, do we know?'

'Clive Thornton.'

Caroline shook her head. 'I knew there was something off about Susan this morning. She couldn't even look us in the eye. How was she last night, Dex?'

'Not that bad. Shocked at first. Inconsolable. But then she just seemed to get on with it. Bit like when she got up and started cleaning the kitchen earlier. It's like a switch had just flipped.'

The interesting choice of words hadn't been lost on Caroline. 'Okay,' she said. 'So let's say for the moment the burglary and the murder are linked. If that's the case, then despite her behaviour being a bit odd, you'd assume she wasn't involved, because otherwise why would they report the burglary?'

'Covering her tracks?' Sara suggested.

'But what would be the point? If she hadn't done that, we'd never know it had happened.'

'Maybe we did need to know it had happened. Perhaps that was the whole point.'

'But why?'

Sara shrugged. 'That's the big question.'

Caroline considered this for a few moments, well aware there had to be an answer, but not wanting to tread on Dexter's toes.

She shook her head. 'No, I don't think we're looking at this in the right way,' she said. 'We're coming up with theories and trying to make the evidence fit. We need to work from the ground up.'

'But that doesn't give us anything,' Aidan replied. 'None of it seems to fit together. It's all so fragmented.'

'Then we strip it right back to basics and we start again. It does all fit together. What we're seeing here is fragments of what happened. These discoveries are real. The pieces all fit. We're just not looking at the right picture on the box.' Caroline looked around her, and she could see her team was already starting to look dejected. 'But first,' she said, 'I'm going to pop out and grab us all a big box of muffins and some proper coffee.'

10

Caroline and Dexter hadn't expected to find themselves back at Susan Thornton's house quite so soon, but the revelation about the recent break-in had thrown up more than a few questions in Caroline's mind.

Susan's son, Ross, was in the kitchen making cups of tea and coffee whilst her daughter, Emma, sat alongside Susan in the living room.

'We just wanted to ask you a few questions about something that's come to light since we last spoke,' Dexter said, opening the exchange. 'We understand you had break-in here recently, is that correct?'

The look Emma gave her mother told them this was the first she'd heard of it.

'Mum?'

'It's fine,' Susan whispered in response.

'What's this all about? What break-in?'

'It was nothing. Just kids messing about. Your dad reported it, but nothing was taken, so we decided to leave it.'

At the very least, Caroline and Dexter noted, Susan Thornton was engaging in some form of conversation.

'Can you talk me through what happened?' Dexter asked, although he'd already read the notes on the police report. 'Were you home at the time?'

'Yes, we both were. It happened in the middle of the night. Clive came down in the morning and discovered the glass in the back door had been smashed, and it looked as though someone had opened the door. There was cash on the side, and all sorts of other things they could have taken, but nothing was gone. We could only presume something had spooked them and they scarpered.'

'Probably Dad's snoring,' Emma said. 'Why didn't you tell me any of this?'

'What's the point?' Susan replied, looking at her. 'We didn't deliberately hide it from you, but nothing was taken and no harm was done, so there's no point anyone worrying.'

'We wouldn't have worried. We would've wanted to help.'

'You're worrying now.'

'No, I'm concerned you didn't tell us. Besides which, it's well known that burglars will often go back to the same property to try again.'

Emma looked at Dexter, as if pleading for moral support.

'She's right. Statistically speaking, if you've been a victim of burglary once, you're far more likely to be a victim again.'

'I wasn't a victim of burglary, because nothing was taken,' Susan replied. 'It was a broken pane of glass, nothing more. There really is no need for all the fuss.'

'And I suppose it was Dad who said don't bother getting the police involved, was it?' Emma asked.

'No, actually. It was me. Your dad was the one who called them in the first place. They said they couldn't send anyone out as nothing had been taken, and that we should get the door replaced. They offered to send us some leaflets and information on increasing security, and said they'd send someone round within the next week to advise us. Then your dad and I had a chat, and we called them back later on to say don't worry, it's better just to leave it.'

'But they'd definitely been in?'

Susan gave a slight shrug. 'We think so. Your dad spotted some muddy shoe prints on the kitchen floor, but I think there's every chance they were his. Not that he'd admit it, of course.'

Ross came into the room with the teas and coffees.

'Did you know about this?' Emma asked him.

'About what?' Ross replied.

'Mum and Dad had a break-in.'

'No. Mum?'

'It's nothing,' Susan replied. 'I was just telling your sister, a couple of weeks back your dad came down in the morning and found one of the panes of glass in the back door had been smashed. Nothing was taken. I don't think anyone even got in. Your dad called the police, then we realised there was probably no point in pursuing anything, and that was that. Now can everyone please just leave it be? We've got enough to deal with right now, without having to spend our time raking over this nonsense.'

Before Caroline or Dexter could speak, Susan stood up and left the room. The sound of footsteps on the staircase told them she was heading upstairs.

Emma gestured towards the door. 'Should we…'

'I'm sure she'll be fine,' Dexter said. 'Perhaps we could speak to the two of you while you're here?'

Ross shrugged. 'You can do, but as you can see we don't know a thing about this break-in, so I'm not sure what we'll be able to do to help.'

'No, that's fine. I was hoping you might be able to tell me a little more about your dad. We like to try to flesh things out as much as possible, to get a full understanding of a person's life. That way, we're much more likely to get closer to finding out who did this.'

'Makes sense, I guess. What do you want to know? I'm pretty sure Mum's already told you everything.'

'It doesn't hurt to go over things again,' Dexter replied. 'Make sure we've covered all bases. He did a lot of charity work, we understand.'

'Yeah. All sorts. I don't know much about it, but he used to use a lot of his business contacts to secure donations, funding, sponsorship, all that sort of thing. Charity auctions and events. He'd even go and volunteer and help out at things, properly show his face. It wasn't just fundraising and connections. He got properly involved.'

'Did he have any particular causes that were close to his heart?'

'All sorts, really. I think he just genuinely liked to help out and do good. He liked to see people happy.'

'Would you say he was a family man?' Dexter asked.

Ross and Emma exchanged a glance.

'I would've said so,' Ross replied, 'but I don't think Emma and I quite see things the same way on that front.'

'I think it feels different being his daughter to being his son,' Emma said.

Dexter cocked his head slightly. 'How do you mean?' he asked.

'I think Dad and I connected better than he did with Emma,' Ross replied, as diplomatically as he could. 'I don't imagine it was anything personal. I think he was just a better dad for a son than he was for a daughter, if that makes sense?'

'I don't have children, but I'll take your word for it,' Dexter said.

Caroline knew instantly what Ross meant. Before she'd had children, she'd always seen herself in her mind's eye with sons rather than daughters. As fate had provided her with two sons, she'd never had the chance to test that theory, but even now she still couldn't imagine herself being a mother to a girl.

'I think it's fair to say it wasn't just that,' Emma added. 'He could be a pretty overbearing person, in his own way.'

'How do you mean?' Dexter asked.

Emma gave a large sigh. 'It's hard to say. He was never loud or threatening, or anything like that. But what he said, went. He was the sort of person who tended to get his own way. I was never someone who put up with that, even as a child.'

Dexter silently confirmed to himself that was the impression Emma had already given him.

'I don't want to paint him out to be a bad man,' Emma continued. 'And I think it's fair to say everyone has their good points and bad points. Their upsides and downsides. But I think maybe I was just a little more receptive to the downsides than a lot of other people. Although I'm sure Mum saw her fair share, too.'

Dexter nodded. 'Doubtless, considering how long they were married. Were there any aspects of his personality you think might have led to the sort of situation where someone might have wanted to kill him?'

'Jesus, no,' Ross replied, almost too instinctively. 'Nothing like that at all.'

Emma, however, seemed a little more reserved.

'I don't think so,' she said. 'Although you can never really know, can you? Like I say, maybe I saw things differently to everyone else. But I've got to say, I quite often felt sorry for Mum.'

Caroline and Dexter exchanged a brief glance. They

both knew from experience that there were the odd occasions where interviewing family members of the deceased could be truly enlightening. And this felt very much like one of those moments.

11

Dexter hadn't expected to find anyone else in the office at that time of the evening. But if he'd been a betting man, his money would have been on Sara Henshaw.

'I think I might have found something,' Sara said, her eyes tired and bloodshot from a long day in front of her computer screen.

'Go on,' Dexter replied, well aware that she had an uncanny knack for finding the missing link in major cases. More often than not, her eye for detail uncovered a vital piece of information that led the team to their killer.

'I've been looking through the CCTV from the castle. From before the power failure, I mean. Just in case there was anything we'd missed. There's something that doesn't quite seem right.' Sara pressed a button on her keyboard, and a video began to play on the screen. 'Have a look at this. It's from three o'clock yesterday afternoon. An hour before Clive Thornton closed the castle, and one of the last times he was seen alive.'

Dexter watched the video, but he wasn't sure what he was meant to be looking at. The only thing of note was a man in a cream-coloured suit and matching fedora, who spent a couple of minutes taking photos of the horseshoes on the walls of the Great Hall before leaving again shortly after.

'Okay,' he said. 'Is this the guy I'm meant to be watching?'

'Yeah. I know what you're thinking. Maybe a little bit strange to walk in, take some photos and walk straight back out again, but hardly suspicious in itself, right?'

'I dunno. That's a pretty dodgy hat he's wearing. The whole outfit's a bit of a worry, if I'm honest.'

Sara laughed. 'I'm with you. But look. This next clip's from the day before, just before eleven in the morning.'

Sara pressed a button and the video started to play. For a few seconds, nothing happened. Then the same man walked into the castle and began looking around. Dexter nodded slowly as he watched him reading a few of the displays and perusing the items for sale in the gift shop. A few moments later, the man looked over at the woman who'd been working on the front desk that day and had engaged him in conversation.

'Can we work out what they're saying?' Dexter asked.

'Not without a lip reader, but I don't think we'll need to,' Sara said, as the man on the video walked over to the front desk and started to write in the visitors' book. 'If we get that, we get his name. Plus we can speak to the member of staff, who might well remember what was said. But from how brief the chat was, I can't imagine it'll be anything more interesting than "Come over here and sign the guestbook, you weird-looking person."'

'Customer service at its finest. No wonder he couldn't refuse. Let's hope the volunteer remembers which name was his.'

'Got that covered,' Sara said with a smile, before taking the video footage back a few minutes. 'Watch this. The old couple here were the previous people to sign the book. And once they'd finished writing out their life story... There we go.'

'Nicely spotted,' Dexter murmured, watching as the volunteer turned the page to start a fresh one, ready for their mystery man in the fedora to arrive a few minutes later.

'That should make it pretty obvious which one's his. It'll be at the top of a page, and with any luck it'll have the date and time written next to it.'

Dexter grinned. 'Bingo. Brilliant work, Sara. Seriously.'

12

Dexter had never been more pleased to have an efficient heater in his car than he was the next morning, sitting in the car park at Oakham Castle, waiting for the building to open.

The moment the door was unlocked, he got out of his car and made his way inside, pleasantly surprised to see the female volunteer from the CCTV footage on the front desk.

'It's good to see you open again so quickly,' he said, introducing himself. 'Can't have been an easy decision to make.'

'Back on the horse, and all that. If you'll excuse the poor taste joke.'

'My favourite kind of joke,' Dexter replied, smiling. 'Sorry, I didn't quite catch your name.'

'Clare. Clare Garner.'

'Lovely to meet you, Clare. Must feel weird being the first one back here.'

'It is a bit. But I guess they needed to get the place open again as quickly as possible. Income for the council.'

'True,' Dexter replied, unsure what else to say. 'Anyway, I just thought I'd come down to wish you all the best on your first day back open. Well done for managing to keep the rumour mill quiet, too. I'm amazed it hasn't ended up all over Facebook.'

Clare smiled and let out a small chuckle. 'You and me both. Never know — could've turned it into one of those ghoulish and macabre tourist attractions. That'd boost the council's coffers quite nicely.'

'They should have you as head of marketing,' Dexter said, taking his phone out of his pocket. 'While I'm here, there was something I wanted to ask. I don't suppose you remember this man visiting the castle recently, do you?'

He passed his phone towards her, a still image of the man in the cream suit and fedora blown up large on the screen.

'Yes, he came in a few days ago. Foreign man. German, I think he was. He didn't seem to know the area all that well, so I presume he was a tourist.'

'Did he say much?'

'Not a whole lot, no. I asked him to sign the visitors' book, then tried to engage him in conversation, as I tend to do when people come in, but he clearly wanted to keep himself to himself.'

'Do you remember what was said?'

Clare curled her lower lip outward and shook her head. 'Not really. I think I asked if he was local, and he said no. I asked if he was staying long and he said he was flying back home late the next evening. His answers were pretty short and sweet, and there were a few people queuing up to pay, so I left him to it.

Dexter considered what Clare had said. The following evening was the night Clive Thornton was murdered. Had this man killed him, knowing he would be on the first flight back home to Germany?

'You mentioned that he signed the visitors' book. Can you show me which one was him?'

'Ooh, I can try,' Clare replied, opening the book. 'Ah, yes, this was him. At the top of this page, here. Andreas Karlsen.'

'Mind if I take a picture?' Dexter asked, holding his phone above the guestbook.

'Not at all. Go ahead.'

Dexter took a photo, then looked at the book more closely. 'Did he do this, too?' he asked, pointing to a capital O, which had been crossed out before being replaced by the name Andreas Karlsen.

'Yes, he must have done. It was a fresh page. He was the first person to write on it.'

Although he didn't yet know what it meant, this didn't sit comfortably with Dexter. Not by a long shot. If this man's name really was Andreas Karlsen, why had he started to write another name, and then crossed it out? Why was he so keen to use a pseudonym in something as innocent as a castle guestbook? And what had made him so nervous that he'd almost given the game away and used his real name?

Dexter didn't know the answers to those questions, but he was now determined to find out.

13

A chill ran down Caroline's spine as Dexter explained the incident with the castle's guestbook. Far from their usual experience of murders resulting from a jealous rage or a failed business deal, this was starting to feel more like a Cold War mystery.

'That is really bloody strange,' she said, as she tried to compute the possibilities. 'And look at the guy. The mysterious stranger in the light suit and hat. It's like some bizarre spy movie.'

'It does feel a bit cliché, doesn't it? But let's look at the facts. Why would he visit the castle two days in a row, only spend a couple of minutes there the second time and only to take photos of the horseshoes? And who the hell gets their own name wrong and has to cross it out?'

'No, I agree. It's definitely an attempt to cover his identity.'

'Explains the hat, too. You can barely see his face with the brim down that low. He knows he won't be identifiable from CCTV, but at the same time a bloke in a hat doesn't look particularly odd to anyone else walking around at the time. And his flight home being only a few hours after Clive Thornton was killed — that's just the icing on the cake.'

'I'd be tempted to agree. What's your next step?' Caroline asked, keen not to make unwarranted suggestions of her own, and for Dexter to take the lead in his own investigation.

'I've got Sara and Aidan ringing round the local hotels to see if any of them had an Andreas Karlsen booked in. Failing that, anyone who fits his description or nationality. Hopefully, we can track him down and find out where he was staying. That way we can look at the hotel's CCTV to get a better look at him, and their booking system should give us his home address and contact details.'

'Excellent stuff,' Caroline replied. 'That's exactly what I would've said. It might be worth speaking to local restaurants and cafés, too. He would've had to have eaten at some point while he was here, and if he used his card we'll be able to trace the details back to him.'

'That's a good point. I'll make sure we get onto that.'

There was a knock at the office door.

'Come in,' Caroline called.

Aidan entered and turned to Dexter. 'Sarge, we've got a positive match on our overseas visitor. Looks like he was staying at the Wisteria Hotel. When I gave the name Karlsen, the guy straightaway mentioned him looking like a cream-coloured cowboy.'

'Well, that sounds promising. Unless there's a Kenny Rogers convention going on that we don't know about.'

'Why are you looking at me?' Caroline asked.

Dexter shrugged. 'Just seems like the sort of thing you might be into.'

'Says the man who brought up Kenny Rogers unprompted. Cheeky git.'

'Have they got contact details for him?' Dexter asked Aidan.

'Yep. Home address, email address and phone number. We've tried calling, but the number's dead.'

'Then it's sounding more and more like this is our man. But if he's given a false name and a false phone number, what are the chances he's given his real address?'

'That's what I thought,' Aidan replied. 'And just to add to the confusion, the home address he's given is in Norway.'

Dexter shook his head. 'This is getting weirder by the minute. What did the staff at the hotel say? Was there anything suspicious about him? Did he say much to them?'

'Not that they mentioned, no. Only that he stood out due to his dress sense, if you can call it that. I looked up the address on Google Maps. It definitely exists, and it's definitely a house. Whether he lives there or not is another matter.'

'Alright. Then we need to liaise with the police in Norway and build a link there. They'll be able to tell us whether Andreas Karlsen is known to them, or whether he really is a registered citizen. Get onto Border Control, too. They'll have a record of him coming in and out of the country — if he's used a passport in that name.'

'Is that going to be any help, though?' Aidan asked.

'How do you mean?' Dexter replied.

'I mean, if he's entered the country, he'll have had to have used a passport. We know he's been trying to mask his identity and using Andreas Karlsen as a pseudonym. So he's either entered the country on a passport with that name, in which case it doesn't help us find out his real identity, or he's entered on either his real name or another pseudonym, which we have no way of knowing other than interrogating the identity of every passenger on every flight into the UK from Norway over the past few weeks. And that's if he flew directly from Norway, and not through another country. And anyway, if he is some sort of spy or something, we'll have no chance of tracking down his true identity because the cover will be watertight, and the Norwegian police aren't exactly going to hand him over to us.'

Caroline murmured her agreement. 'There's the potential for a real diplomatic conundrum here. This could go way above our heads. It's one thing fighting off EMSOU to keep control of a case, but if this is what we think it is, we're looking at the Met wading in with Counter Terrorism Command.'

'Worst case scenario,' Dexter added.

Caroline gave a slight nod. 'We've always got to consider all possibilities.'

Dexter perched on the edge of the desk and steepled his hands in front of his face. 'Okay, so let's just say for one minute that some mysterious stranger has flown in from Norway purely to carry out an elaborate and highly risky murder in Oakham Castle, before flying straight back home again. Even if we ignore how absolutely barmy that sounds, it still leaves one enormous gaping question. Why?'

In the absence of a response, Dexter continued. 'Why on earth would the Norwegian Secret Services, for Christ's sake, want to bump off a Rutlander who's spent his life dedicating all his spare time to charities and good causes?'

'Maybe it was a cover,' Aidan replied. 'The perfect opportunity to come across as a good person, but all the time he was some sort of secret agent.'

'What, all the time sitting in Rutland, spying against that famous behemoth of espionage, Norway? Come on.'

Caroline raised her hands. 'I think the most important thing right now is to focus on the facts, and to keep our minds focused on what we *do* know. And that doesn't include spies, secret agents or the lovechild of James Bond and Kenny Rogers. Let the evidence and the facts lead you to the story. Not the other way round. Let's keep our feet on terra firma, here.'

Dexter nodded his agreement. 'We need to gather more information. Let's speak to Border Control and the police in Norway. Find out if Andreas Karlsen exists, find out who he is, and find out if we can interview him. We'll learn a lot by the reaction we get from the authorities over there.'

14

Caroline walked into Chief Superintendent Derek Arnold's office feeling as hopeful, hopeless, energetic and listless as she ever did. Although she always came in with hopes of a positive outcome and a desire for progress, it never quite came in the way she expected.

Arnold was often full of pleasant surprises, but she'd recently realised these often came in the form of lip service and meaningless platitudes, designed to placate her in the face of deftly side-swerving each of her reasonable requests and any concerns she happened to raise. This was how he'd managed to reach the position he had, she supposed. Perhaps he was just perfect management material.

'What's the latest?' he asked her, as vaguely as he ever did.

'On Operation Titan? Still moving. We've had a couple of interesting developments. It turns out Clive and

Susan Thornton had a break-in at their property recently, which they reported and then NFA'd. Nothing taken, presumed to be kids or opportunists who got spooked and legged it. Weirdest thing is they didn't tell either of their kids, and Mrs Thornton didn't think to mention it when we first spoke to her.'

'Maybe she didn't think it was connected.'

'Perhaps. But you'd imagine being the victim of crime twice in a short space of time might link up in your mind somehow. In any case, our most interesting lead at the moment is a man seen on CCTV at the castle in the days leading up to Clive's murder. He visited twice — once very shortly before Clive was killed — and appears to have used a pseudonym in the castle's visitor book. He started writing one name, then crossed it out and wrote another. Who on earth forgets their own name? He was dressed pretty unusually, too, in a light-coloured suit and fedora, like some sort of heavenly cowboy or one of those characters you see in casinos in Las Vegas.'

'Not doing a very good job of blending in in Rutland, then, was he?' Arnold asked.

'Might've done better the week of the Burghley Horse Trials, but I imagine he'd still stand out a mile.'

'Spelling his own name wrong in the guestbook isn't exactly the most covert manoeuvre either, is it?'

'Very true,' Caroline replied.

'So what makes us think he might be connected in some way? Because from what I've heard so far, he sounds more like the comedy diversion than a reasonable suspect.'

'A few things,' Caroline replied, giving Arnold a taste of his own vague medicine. 'It's difficult to pin it down specifically, but there are a number of things that don't quite make sense. We're looking into him as a person of interest and will report back with anything of note, but the timings and a few of the details are making us wonder. Speaking of wondering, sir, I was going to ask if you had any news on that extra body we're drafting in. Has the transfer gone through yet?'

'It has indeed,' Arnold replied, leaning back in his chair with a proud look on his face. 'You'll be pleased to know I've literally just had the confirmation paperwork through a few moments ago. Your new team member arrives the day after tomorrow.'

'Really? That's excellent news, sir. Tell me more.'

'His name's Elijah Drummond, a Detective Sergeant who's been posted with EMSOU for the last couple of years. Very highly thought of up there, apparently. They've got big hopes for him in the future.'

'That's good,' Caroline replied. 'So why are they sending him to us?'

Arnold shrugged. 'Extra experience, I guess. It's a very different environment here to EMSOU, so he'll be a more rounded officer for it.'

'How long will we have him for?' Caroline asked.

'To be confirmed. I'll have to keep the higher-ups updated as we go along. They'll want to see we're making good use of the budget, and all that jazz. Everything has to be justified on an ongoing basis. You know how it is.'

Caroline nodded. She knew only too well how it was.

'I've just got the one question, sir,' she said. 'Why are they sending us a DS? Isn't that a bit overkill? The team's already fifty percent DS and above.'

Arnold gave another shrug. 'Can't complain, really. They could've sent some wet-behind-the-ears DC who's been out of uniform thirty seconds. Having more experienced officers on the team can't be a bad thing.'

Caroline chose her words carefully. In her experience, resources very rarely landed in your lap as it was — it certainly wasn't normal to be given more than you'd asked for.

'I just wondered if it might make things a little lopsided,' she said. 'There'll be more management than there are people to manage.'

'Maybe they're opening the door to the possibility of expanding things even further. Who knows? This time next year you could have two extra constables on your team.'

'With the greatest of respect, sir, I very much doubt it.'

'Me too. But in any case, I'm not going to argue. Never look a gift horse in the mouth, Caroline. Certainly not in this job, anyway.'

Caroline pursed her lips and nodded.

15

Both Caroline and Dexter had been left with a distinctly uneasy feeling after they'd last spoken to Susan Thornton and her children. It seemed both Ross and Emma had very different opinions of their dad. If Emma had been willing to voice those differences in the way she already had, it seemed logical there must be more under the surface that could be of use to the investigation.

They'd arranged to meet Emma on her own at Hungry Birds, a coffee shop in the middle of Oakham, and they'd managed to secure a table in the corner, where Emma would be able to speak freely without the formality of a police interview room. Quite often, where sensitive subjects were involved, they found witnesses or family members would clam up in a more formal environment, and Caroline had always been a big fan of using the most effective method to gain information, even if it was less conventional.

Emma seemed more nervous than she had the last couple of times they'd met her, and Caroline wondered how much of it was due to the fact she was no longer in the family home with her mother and brother beside her. She'd seemed confident and forthright enough before, though, and Caroline had no doubt she'd be talking in no time at all.

'Thank you for agreeing to meet up with us today,' she said, smiling at Emma. 'I know it must be difficult having to keep talking about things, especially so soon after your father's death. I promise you we really are trying to be as sensitive to that as possible.'

'I know,' Emma replied quietly. 'If it helps catch whoever did this, that can only be a good thing.'

'That's our aim. And we're certainly doing all we can on that front. The reason we wanted to speak to you on your own today was because last time we spoke, you intimated your dad hadn't been quite the saint a lot of other people made him out to be. I know no-one's perfect and all humans are complex, but we just wanted to get a little more detail on that side of your dad. It might sound unlikely, but it's possible there could be something there that might open up a new thread for the investigation, or even tie together a couple of existing ones. Like you say, anything that might help us catch whoever did this. Now, you'd be surprised at some of the things that can unlock a case, so please don't hold anything back because you think it won't be useful. That could stop us catching your father's killer. And we all want the same thing here.'

Emma nodded, but didn't say a word.

Caroline looked at Dexter, who opened with the first of the questions they'd prepared.

'Emma, you mentioned your dad used to treat you differently to the way he treated Ross. Why do you think that is?'

Emma gave a slight shrug. 'Because I was a girl.'

'Was that really his way of thinking?' Dexter asked. 'Do you think he saw girls differently to the way he saw boys?'

'Oh, definitely. It was obvious in the way he spoke to me and Ross. I don't think he ever said anything that outright proved his opinions, but it was pretty clear to see. In a way, he never needed to say anything.'

'You also mentioned that you used to feel sorry for your mum. What did you mean by that?'

'Well, she's a woman too. That automatically meant she didn't get as much respect as a man would've done. Again, there was nothing explicit. More just a general lack of respect. Maybe he was just a bit old-school in that sense. Perhaps I took it personally because I was a girl and I was on the receiving end of it all.'

'I don't think you need to make excuses for anyone else's behaviour,' Dexter replied. 'If that's the way he was, and that's the way it made you feel, then nothing else matters. Can you give me some examples of the sorts of things you mean, though? It's difficult for us to understand without knowing what you class as disrespectful.'

Emma let out a sigh and sat back in her chair. 'I guess

things like asking Ross where he wanted to go for dinner, or what he wanted to watch on TV, but never asking me or Mum. Or that I'd get told off for doing something as a kid, but if Ross did the exact same thing the next day, Dad wouldn't say a word.'

'Did that create any animosity between you and your brother?'

'At the time, probably. But nothing long-term. We get on really well now, even if we do tend to see things pretty differently. We're both pretty well-rounded adults, I think.'

Dexter nodded as he took this in and digested it. 'And would you say your dad's style, for want of a better word, spilled over into other walks of life? Is it possible he might have upset someone else with his ways of doing things?'

Emma seemed to think about this for a moment. 'I don't know,' she said eventually. 'I mean, it's possible. Outside of the house he tended to be much better at putting the act on. He knew what he had to do to come across the right way. He wouldn't have got as far as he did, and been as respected as he was, if he hadn't known where to draw the line. But if you're asking me whether I can think of any specific examples or people, then I'm afraid not. Sorry. I'd love to be more help than this, but if I'm honest I think it was just a home life thing. I certainly don't think it was anything that'd make someone want to kill him, if that's what you're asking.'

Dexter looked briefly at Caroline. Neither of them needed to say a word, but the meaning was clear: this appeared to be another dead end.

16

Dexter had barely lifted the coffee mug to his lips to take the first sip when Sara called over to him.

'Sarge, come and take a look at this.'

He stood up and made his way over to Sara's desk.

'We've been focusing on looking through the business and financial records,' she said. 'Financial investigators are combing through everything as we speak. In the meantime, I've been doing a bit of research of my own, and I found this news article hidden away in the depths of the internet.'

Sara clicked her mouse, and a browser window appeared on the screen in front of her. Dexter leaned forward and read the article with growing interest.

It was relatively brief, and the translation into English provided by Google was tricky to decipher at certain points, but its importance was clear. It detailed how a planned hydropower initiative in Norway had been put on hold after one of the companies associated had withdrawn their involvement at the last minute, having discovered concerns. There was a strong statement from a minister in the Norwegian government, castigating the overseas company for effectively collapsing the whole deal at the eleventh hour, after years of painstaking political and economic work to build one of the largest renewable energy initiatives in Northern Europe. The article didn't make clear why the company had pulled out, but it did briefly name them. Dexter recognised it immediately.

'That was one of Clive Thornton's companies, wasn't it?' he asked, already knowing the answer.

Sara nodded. 'Yep. Obviously we've no idea what actually happened, and this is the only reference I can find to it at all, other than the initial announcements in the Norwegian press about the plans. But they don't mention Clive Thornton's firm or give us any information about what might have gone wrong. It does explain why the Norwegian government might have been more than a little upset with him, though. We're talking tens of billions here. I've no idea how much of that Clive Thornton's firm would've seen. It could have been next to nothing. But the article seems to suggest the collapse of the entire deal hinged on him pulling out. It seems to have caused quite a stir.'

'Well, well, well,' Dexter replied. 'It looks like you've done it again, Sara.'

17

Caroline tried to steer the overly laden shopping trolley around the corner of the aisle, doing her best to avoid her fellow shoppers' ankles as Mark shepherded Josh and Archie along behind.

She wasn't sure why she'd agreed to turn the weekly shop into a family outing — something Mark had read online about improving family cohesion by getting everybody involved — but she could feel her stress levels rising before they'd even got out of the fruit and veg section.

'Mum, can we get donuts?' Josh asked, at a volume that would have been communicable had Caroline been in a completely different supermarket.

'Maybe,' she replied noncommittally. 'And can we please stop shouting?'

'And chocolate,' Archie followed up. '*Loads* of chocolate.'

'We've got plenty of sweets and chocolate in the cupboard at home,' Caroline replied.

'Dad, can we get donuts and chocolate?' Josh asked.

'I think your mum's already answered that.'

'I know, but *please*.'

'She's still answered it, mate. It doesn't matter how many times you ask. You've got a maybe. That's pretty good for her. I wouldn't push it and turn it into a no.'

Caroline felt fortunate she had her back to Mark. That way, he couldn't see the look on her face.

A little later on, as Josh and Archie were perusing the magazines, she felt the time was right to pounce.

'*That's pretty good for her?*' she asked.

'Hmmm?'

'Don't undermine me in front of the kids, Mark. Saying "maybe" isn't "pretty good" for me. It's realistic, it's accurate and it keeps them quiet for a bit. What would you prefer I'd done? Shut them down immediately, or signed a donut promise in blood?'

'What's this all about, Caz? I don't know what you're talking about.'

'Come on, you do. Don't make me out to be the big bad wolf. We're meant to be a team. A united front. Don't go playing good cop to my bad cop. Please.'

Mark raised his hands in mock surrender. 'Alright. It was only meant to be a joke. A bit of lighthearted relief. I didn't mean anything by it.'

Caroline quietly accepted his apology, gathered the boys and continued down the aisles of the supermarket.

A few minutes later, her phone buzzed, a text message on the screen from Dexter. She could see the first sentence or two before the preview cut off, and it seemed to be something to do with Operation Titan. She paused for a moment and opened the message.

Sara's done some more digging and found gold — surprise surprise. Turns out Thornton had links to a failed business deal in Norway. A big one too. Government contract, renewable energy, millions and billions of pounds at stake. Looks like the Norwegians blamed him for the deal falling through. Will brief Arnold. Sounds like a pretty big motive, no?

She locked her phone and put it back in her pocket. That was the sort of message that was going to take her some time to digest, and which didn't need an immediate response.

'Work?' Mark asked.

'Yeah,' she replied, with a gesture that made out the message had been a pure inconvenience. 'But it can wait until tomorrow. I should've just left the thing at home.'

Mark smiled. 'One step at a time, eh?'

Caroline scoffed, humoured. 'Cheeky sod. I'm not some recovering addict.'

'Mmmm. You keep telling yourself that.'

'Alright,' she replied with a smile, picking up the pace and moving the trolley forwards. 'Just for that,

I'm buying extra donuts. Who's the big bad wolf now?'

18

Caroline observed from a distance as Dexter took centre stage at another briefing on Operation Titan. With the incident room being so small, the only other option that'd make her feel as if she wasn't interfering would have been to have disappeared each time Dexter held a briefing. That would have looked even more odd, she thought, so she'd opted to keep quiet and watch from a distance, keen to hear the various bits of information pulled together, and proud to see him fully in control of leading the investigation.

It felt good to be taking a back seat. She was there if Dexter needed her, and was happy to get as involved as he wanted her to be, but — crucially — she'd handed over the heavy weight of responsibility, and it was an added relief to see Dexter handling it so confidently. She couldn't lie that there was still a large part of her that missed the pressure in some way, but that was more than offset by the reduced stress in her life.

'The main development from a forensic point of view,' Dexter said as Caroline tuned back in, 'is the pathology report. It confirms there were no sedatives in Clive Thornton's system at the time of death, and no signs of any poisoning at all. To me, that throws up more questions than answers. We know Clive didn't put up much of a struggle against his killer. We've had confirmation that there's a very high probability the weapon used to kill Clive was the horseshoe in question. The size and shape of the indentations appear to match, and flecks of white paint were identified. We'd need to find the horseshoe to confirm a definite match, but it looks highly likely at this moment in time. There was no skin under his fingernails, no signs of bruising on his arms or any of the other typical signs we'd expect. All we've got is some slight marking on his upper wrists, where it seems they were bound to the chair. It's nowhere near what we'd expect from a proper struggle, though. Certainly not if he thought his life was in danger. So if he didn't think his life was in danger at that point, it seems to indicate a much higher likelihood that Clive Thornton knew his killer.'

Aidan raised his hand, and Dexter indicated for him to speak.

'That doesn't fit in with what we know of Karlsen though, does it?'

Dexter let out a loud sigh. 'No, it doesn't. We've nothing yet to indicate the two men knew each other personally, and even if they did, based on what we know about the hydropower initiative and the trouble that caused, it seems likely that Clive Thornton would've realised his life was in danger and put up much more of a struggle. The lack of sedatives in his system does throw a pretty big spanner in the works there, I agree. But all we can do is go by the evidence in front of us,' he said, glancing across at Caroline, who gave a barely perceptible smile, before the ringing of her phone called her back to her office.

Dexter continued. 'Maybe we've let ourselves get a bit too carried away with theories and fantasies. That's not to say those theories are wrong — they could well be right — but we need to work from the bottom up rather than the top down, or all we'll do is waste time and reduce our chances of getting justice for Clive's family.'

19

Caroline closed her office door behind her and picked up the phone.

'Caroline Hills.'

'Hi, it's Leah MacGregor calling from the Rutland & Stamford Mercury.'

Caroline's heart sank as she heard the words. It was possible there could be an entirely innocent explanation as to why Leah MacGregor was calling her, but instinctively she knew the timing was no coincidence and that it had to be connected with Operation Titan. So far, they'd managed to keep the mob at bay, but she had a feeling that wouldn't be the case for much longer.

'Hi, Leah. How can I help you?' she said, trying to sound as friendly and positive as possible.

'I'm not sure,' Leah replied. 'Bit of an odd one, this. We've heard a rumour about a body being found in Oakham Castle recently. Is that true?'

'Leah, you know I can't comment on the existence or otherwise of cases, but I can promise you that if anything had happened, and if we were in a position to announce anything or needed any assistance from our good friends in the local media, we'd call you immediately.'

'So it is true?'

Caroline sighed. 'No, I didn't say that. I said if it was true, and if it would be beneficial to do so, we'd have contacted you already.'

'But you haven't, which means you don't think it would be beneficial.'

'Or it didn't happen. You know our policy is to neither confirm nor deny.'

'And ours is to keep the public informed, and to ensure that local people feel safe on the streets.'

Caroline gritted her teeth. 'That's very much our main focus too. In fact, some people might say we're considered to be the experts in how best to do that.'

'Yes. Some might. Is it true that you're on the hunt for a mysterious foreigner, who might be connected with the killing?'

Caroline let out a laugh — one she hoped would be suitably convincing. 'Who told you that?' she asked.

'You know any journalist will always protect their sources,' Leah replied.

'Then I think you need to work on getting some new sources.'

'So you're saying it isn't true? Can I put that on the record?'

'Come on, Leah. You're a bright woman. You know what "neither confirm nor deny" means. I know you want a good story. And I know you have the public's best interests at heart. But we really do have far more experience in how to make sure that happens. I don't think speculative stories and listening to the rumour mill is going to help anyone. All that does is fuel anxieties and stoke fear in local communities where it really isn't needed.'

Leah MacGregor fell silent for a few moments before speaking.

'You'll call me when you have anything?' she asked. 'Before anyone else?'

'Before anyone else,' Caroline agreed.

With the call ended, Caroline sat back in her chair and tried to calm her breathing. She had no idea how that information had got to the reporter, or who had decided to spill the beans, but it really didn't make any difference. If she had to pick a favourite, experience told her it was likely that a member of staff from the hotel quite innocently mentioned to a not-altogether-trustworthy friend or family member that the police had been to visit, creating fuel and a catalyst for the local rumour mill. For now, her main focus on that front had to be on making sure MacGregor kept her story out of print — at least for the time being. If they were ever going to find the man known to them as Andreas Karlsen, they could do without him being forced even further underground.

Barely a minute after she'd finished speaking to Leah MacGregor, Caroline's phone rang again. Despite her assumptions, caller ID told her it wasn't MacGregor at the other end.

'Caroline Hills,' she said, as she answered the call.

'Caroline, Derek Arnold here,' the Chief Superintendent replied. 'How's the hunt for Karlsen coming along?'

'We're getting there, slowly but surely. We've put in a request to the Norwegian police, and are also trying to liaise with Border Control to narrow down his whereabouts and uncover his real identity.'

'Okay. Sounds promising. I suppose there's a chance someone'll need to go over there, is there?'

The thought had briefly crossed Caroline's mind, but she didn't see how that would even be feasible, considering the restricted resources. It was usual for overseas trips to happen in pairs.

'I'm not sure, sir. I doubt it'll be necessary, and even if it were, losing half the investigation team for a day or two would be far from ideal.'

'You're not strictly on the investigation team,' Arnold said.

Caroline hadn't expected to feel the reaction she had. His words had not only been perfectly innocent; they were also true. It took a moment for her instinctive reaction to subside and the real meaning of what he was saying to become clear.

'Me?' she asked. 'You think I should go?'

'I don't see why not. You know more than enough about the case, you're an experienced Senior Investigating Officer and you don't have two Detective Sergeants on the team, so we're not exactly blessed with options.'

'Sir, are you suggesting I go with DS Antoine? That'll leave the incident room staffed by two Detective Constables.'

'It'll only be for a matter of hours, and it might not even be necessary. It's all hypothetical for now,' Arnold replied. 'It's not as if they're children. Anyway, they'll have DS Drummond with them.'

'With respect, sir, they haven't even met him yet.'

'And in many other forces across the country, officers on a major investigation might not have ever met any of their team before. What are your other options? Take your two biggest foot soldiers away from the office and the work they're so good at? Say hello to DS Drummond then pop him on a plane to Norway?'

Caroline clenched her teeth. Yet again, Arnold had managed to weasel his way into position and box her in the corner. Annoyingly, though, she knew he was right.

20

He closed the front door of his flat and pulled the security chain across. It was a simple gesture, but one he'd always found symbolic. This side of the locked door, he could temporarily relieve his own security of its duties.

Here, he didn't have to pretend. He didn't have to maintain the act. The jollities and jovialities could be put to one side for a short while, giving him the opportunity to regain the energy he needed to do it all again tomorrow.

It was draining. Day after day, week after week. Logic dictated it should get easier with practice, but it never did. If anything, he only got more tired of the whole charade. While the mask was on, everything was fine. He'd even convinced himself. But the downtime was essential, and that was when reality hit hardest.

It was never intended to be the whole plan. It was always a means to an end — fake it til you make it — in the vain hope that it'd open doors to true happiness. But those hopes were dwindling with every passing day.

He sat down on the sofa and switched on the TV. It wasn't exactly his idea of fun, but it often provided enough of a distraction and kept him occupied for a couple of hours until the need for sleep took over. But tonight that didn't feel like enough.

He'd felt a growing sense over the past few weeks that things were only heading one way. It wasn't overly dramatic for him to think that way. After all, it wasn't the first time.

For as long as he could remember, there had been an innate acceptance within him as to how it would all end. It had never seemed to be a question — just a knowledge that it was the way things had to be. He'd never felt bound by that, or even particularly concerned for the most part. It had simply just been — as much as his hair colour or his name.

Sometimes — in better times — he wondered whether that knowledge and acceptance had reduced his strength somehow, and if he'd be able to put up as much of a fight against himself if he succumbed to the inevitability. But the more he thought about it, the more he knew that wasn't the case.

Strength had never been his weakness, so to speak. He certainly didn't lack it. He'd spent his life pretending to be someone he wasn't. Even actors got days off or breaks between shows. He didn't. It was all day every day, aside from the small moments he got to himself. Alone.

The concept of loneliness had always intrigued him. He found it was completely unconnected to whether you were physically with anybody. He could be in a room full of people and still feel like the loneliest person on Earth. He'd always envied those who found comfort in their own company and who never felt lonely, even though they were alone.

The truth was, nothing had ever felt as if it was enough. He'd accepted for a while now that he was incapable of ever being happy. He couldn't even define what would make him happy, give his life purpose. The whole thing just felt so completely pointless.

That wasn't to say his life had been wasted. He'd been proud, proud that he'd managed to keep this darkness away from his friends and family, proud that he'd protected those people who didn't need to see this side of him. Because deep down he knew there was nothing they could do to help. It was inevitable. Why prolong their agony?

He'd been at this point many times before. On the first few occasions, it had been merely thoughts. Then there'd been the times where he'd made plans. More recently, there'd been the two occasions where he'd mucked it up. Most recently, mixing up grams with milligrams when calculating the number of sleeping tablets he'd need for his body weight had meant a particularly groggy week and a couple of days off work, but he hadn't regretted the act — only the failure.

This time, he wouldn't be so stupid.

He switched off the television and stood up, making his way over to the safe he'd installed inside one of the cupboards in his kitchenette. He unlocked it, and looked at the contents within. The three most valuable items in his life: his birth certificate, his passport and his noose.

He couldn't recall whether he'd done it deliberately, but it seemed almost poetic seeing them lined up from left to right. Birth to death. Beginning to end.

He took the rope in his hand and removed it from the safe, locking the door shut. Standing on a kitchen stool, he loosened the two ceiling tiles and fed the free end of the rope over the steel joist above, tying the knot he'd already tied a thousand times in his mind.

He thought back to when he'd calculated the drop required to break his neck and kill him instantly, recalling the strange feeling of comfort he'd had when he realised he could do it in his own home. The fact these flats had previously been old Victorian buildings hadn't factored into his reasons for living here, but the tall, reinforced ceilings — inexplicably covered with the soulless polystyrene tiles you'd expect in an insurance call centre — had been something of a godsend for him.

He slipped the noose over his neck and stood with his arms by his side. Sweep the feet forwards — or backwards — and knock the stool over. Then it'll all be done. It was the ending he'd written.

The flat lit up blue as his phone rang on the kitchen work surface in front of him. Even from here, through tear-stained eyes, he could see the word on the screen.

Mum.

Swallowing hard, he removed the noose from his neck and climbed down from the stool, his heart hammering in his chest.

He answered the phone. 'Hi, Mum. How's things?'

The familiar voice at the other end of the phone seemed a world away, oblivious to what it had just interrupted.

'I'm fine, Dexter. And how are you?'

21

Taking the morning briefing back to basics wasn't a bad idea, in general. It was common for officers to get so bogged down in the details or specific aspects of a case, that an occasional refresh could often focus minds and serve as a reminder as to what was at the core of their investigation. In the case of that morning's briefing, though, the benefit was mostly for DS Elijah Drummond.

He'd walked into the incident room with an air of confidence that Dexter considered to be a little on the arrogant side, but he couldn't quite put his finger on why. As far as first impressions went, he seemed to have had an almost instantaneous effect on Sara Henshaw, who appeared to be quite taken with him.

Dexter watched as Sara laughed and giggled at everything Drummond said, having left her professionalism at the door entirely. Then again, he could see why. Drummond was tall, well-built and had piercing blue eyes that offset his perfectly-styled dark hair. There was no doubting he was an attractive bloke, and Dexter was sure Drummond knew it, too.

'Okay, let's get cracking, boys and girls,' Dexter said as he made his way to the front of the room. 'This is today's morning briefing on Operation Titan, the investigation into the murder of Clive Thornton. Clive was a retired businessman and an active volunteer working at Oakham Castle. Clive closed the castle to visitors at four o'clock on Monday afternoon, and wasn't seen again until his body was discovered shortly before six o'clock by an events organiser who arrived at the castle to set up for a do the following day. When she entered, the lights and power were all off, as the main fuse had either been tripped or switched off deliberately.'

'If it had been tripped by a fault, wouldn't it have been isolated to the specific fuse? It wouldn't knock out the lights and power,' Drummond interrupted.

'It's usual to put your hand up if you'd like to speak,' Dexter replied, trying not to show his irritation.

'Ah. Right. I just thought, maybe with it being —'

'No no. It's the same as everywhere. I'll take note of what you said about the fuse, but it's largely irrelevant as we believe it was shut off deliberately. It happened within seconds of Clive Thornton locking the doors, as evidenced by the time the CCTV system cut out. Yes, Elijah,' Dexter said, spotting Drummond's hand in the air.

'Did the CCTV system not have battery backup?'

'No. Ambo was called by the events organiser, and they

requested police assistance. Clive's death was caused by multiple blunt force trauma to the skull, which we believe to have been delivered by an ornamental horseshoe, one of which is missing from the wall directly above where Clive's body was found. We're yet to recover the horseshoe, but have good reason to believe that was the murder weapon due to the forensics report, and the fact it can be seen in its place on the wall when viewing the CCTV footage around closing time that day. Two hours later it was gone, and so was a large part of Clive Thornton's skull. CCTV footage from earlier that day shows a man we've identified as Andreas Karlsen — a name we believe to be a pseudonym — visiting the castle, as he had the previous day also. His behaviour seems out of the ordinary, and we believe he flew back to Norway within hours of Clive's death. We've since established that Clive had previous business links to Norway, and his company had been involved in a large national hydropower initiative that the Norwegian government had been trying to implement. When Clive's company pulled out at the last minute, the project collapsed and is predicted to have cost the Norwegian government a considerable sum of money.' Dexter stopped speaking, having spotted a familiar hand in the air. 'Yes. DS Drummond.'

'How was the man identified as Andreas Karlsen?' Drummond asked.

'That's the name he wrote in the visitors' book at the castle.'

'But we think it's a pseudonym?'

'Yes.'

'Why?'

'Because he started to write another name first, but crossed it out. We believe he let his cover slip momentarily.'

'Is that likely? If we're talking about a spy or contract killer, I mean. If he's literally visiting the location where he intends to murder someone, having been sent across Europe to do it, I'd say he's probably very much in work mode and would be unlikely to have made such a basic slip-up, no?'

'We're going by the evidence in front of us,' Dexter replied, starting to become increasingly irritated with Drummond.

'But if he was—'

'We're waiting to hear back from the Norwegian police today,' Dexter continued, cutting Drummond off sharply. 'We'll be able to judge from their response whether there's something darker at play here, and yes, we're compiling documentation ready to hand over to the Met and Counter Terrorism Command should our worst suspicions be confirmed. It's always important to be aware of our role, and to know when to take a back seat. The only other thing to add right now is that we've already had the press sniffing round this yesterday afternoon. We think we've held them at bay for now, but we need to make sure that firstly we keep it that way, and secondly that we are able to control the narrative if they do go to print or if the rumour mill starts to get out of hand. This appears to have been a targeted attack and an isolated event, and we have absolutely no reason to believe that any member of the public is in any danger whatsoever. That said, it shouldn't lessen our resolve in getting justice for Clive Thornton and his family. He was a good man.'

Dexter looked around the room. He could tell his colleagues had as much confidence in that statement as he did. Try as they might, they all knew there had to be more to it than met the eye.

22

'Thoughts?' Caroline asked as Dexter walked into her office and closed the door behind him. Although she could already tell from his reaction in the briefing what Dexter was thinking, she was looking forward to hearing it in his own words.

In the time she'd known Dexter, she'd never seen him be upset or angry about anything, but Elijah Drummond appeared to have found his trigger points within minutes of arriving.

'It's got to be some sort of joke, hasn't it? Bloke's on a wind-up. You can see why EMSOU were so bloody keen to get rid of him,' he said, as he paced the floor in Caroline's office. 'And I'm not surprised they were so confident it might be a permanent move. This'll be the one time the higher-ups keep their word on things like that, I can tell you. Can we just tell them we don't bloody want him?'

Caroline sympathised, but she didn't have many options. 'We've fought tooth and nail to get just one extra team member, Dex. We can't turn around now and say "Sorry, we don't like that one". He's new. He's probably just nervous and trying to make a good impression.'

Dexter shook his head. 'You know that's not the case. He's rude, he's arrogant. He butts in wherever he likes, without a thought for anyone else.'

'Dex, he's been here five minutes.'

'Exactly, and I already want to throttle him. He thinks he knows it all. He's picking holes in the way we do things, trying to make us look like idiotic country bumpkins.'

'Maybe he's just offering an alternative viewpoint. It's good to make sure we've considered all possibilities. There's no harm in having a fresh pair of eyes cast over things. Perhaps there *are* things we need to change or adapt slightly.'

'What, so we end up doing things the exact same way as EMSOU? Then what would be the point of us? They'd swallow us up in seconds. Being able to do things differently is the only thing that keeps this shop open. We wouldn't have half the success rate we do if this was all done by EMSOU.'

Caroline sighed. 'You don't know that, Dex. No-one does. EMSOU have infinitely more resources than we'll ever have. Not to mention staff numbers.'

'More people doesn't mean more gets done, though, does it? I think we're living proof of that. Huge teams just create bloat. Things get lost and forgotten about. People hide in crowds and don't pull their weight. That's why Elijah Drummond stands out like a sore thumb over here. Maybe they weren't trying to get rid of him, after all. You know, I reckon he might genuinely be the best they've got. And that says it all.'

Caroline kept silent for a few moments before speaking.

'Dex, is everything okay?' she asked.

Dexter stopped pacing and stood with his hands on his hips, his head slightly cocked to one side.

'No, it isn't. He's winding me right up.'

'I don't mean Elijah. I mean in general.'

'Yeah. Fine. Why?'

'Because you're not the sort of person to get so wound up about someone else. It's not like you.'

Dexter loosened his tight jaw, moving it from side to side before speaking. 'Yeah, well it's not like you to be defending EMSOU and saying we'd be better off as a part of them.'

'I didn't say that, Dex.'

'Sounded like it.'

'Dexter, you know I want my team to be able to come to me with anything. Anything. And you know I prefer to chip in at the mucky end and I hate pulling rank, so I'm giving you a gentle little reminder that in this office I'm your superior officer, and that commands a certain level of respect. And yes, now I've said that I want to stick my fingers down my throat and vomit. If you need to rant at me, feel free. That's what I'm here for. But if you want to rant *about* me to my face, let's at least do it over a couple of pints in the pub, alright?'

Dexter looked at her and nodded, seeming to come down from his perch a little.

'Yeah. Sorry,' he said. 'I don't know why, but he just winds me up so much.'

Caroline couldn't help but smile. 'He's not that bad. Just a bit enthusiastic. Don't forget he's come from a completely different environment. He's probably used to having to put on an act to get heard above all the other loudmouths over at EMSOU. He'll soon pick up that he doesn't need to do that here.'

'He's a DS, boss. He knows the score. He must get that you don't just walk into a small team like this, where everyone knows everyone, and trample all over it. That's not a cultural thing. That's just being human.'

'To be fair, I have heard they're a different species over there.'

'In that case maybe we should put him in a cage.'

Caroline laughed. 'I doubt it'll come to that. He probably just needs a bit of training.'

'Like one of those dogs you see on the telly, where the owners bring in some mad expert who whips them into shape because the dog keeps eating their shoes in the night.'

'I was thinking more a gentle nudge in the right direction, but I get your point. Do you want me to have a word?'

Dexter took a breath and considered this for a

moment, then let out a loud sigh. 'Nah,' he said. 'It's alright. It's probably just me being over-sensitive. Like you say, I'm sure he'll calm down in good time. He's just over-keen.'

'Nothing wrong with being keen, Dex. Rather that than have him sitting there with his feet up, doing nothing.'

'True. Hey, maybe we can use him as our little Rottweiler puppy. Put all that energy into something useful.'

'I think that's probably enough of the dog comparisons. Before we know it you'll have given us all breeds to match our personalities, and I really don't want to know what mine is. In all seriousness, keep an eye on Elijah. Not in a suspicious way. I mean in a caring one.'

'Caring?' Dexter asked.

'Yeah. The ones who waltz in with that sort of bravado are usually the ones who are the most shy. Someone who's truly confident and sure of themselves doesn't feel the need to hammer it home to everyone else. They just get on with it. If it helps you feel any better, you'll likely find Elijah Drummond doesn't feel all that self-confident at all. He's probably just a shy and anxious little boy who's trying too hard to impress.'

Dexter gave a smile that bordered on a smirk. 'You know, that does make me feel a bit better. I know it's bad to say it, but it does.'

'It's not bad at all. Just human,' Caroline replied. 'We all spend too long judging other people and getting it wrong. Live and let live. Assume the best in people. If you're always trying to do your best and occasionally, innocently, getting it wrong, then you'll find that's what other people are doing too. No-one else is a robot or a bit-part player. Everyone's living their own story in their own world.'

Dexter raised his eyebrows. 'Getting a bit deep and philosophical for this time of the morning, aren't we?'

Caroline shrugged. 'Maybe. But I've picked up enough about people and life in general over the past few years. Worry less, Dex. You don't often let stuff get to you, and I don't think Elijah Drummond should be any different. There are two ways of looking at it. Either he's just shy and anxious, in which case it's best to give him the benefit of the doubt, or he's actually a complete and utter tool, in which case he isn't worth your time getting angry and frustrated over. Whichever way you look at it, it isn't worth the headspace.'

'Wise words,' Dexter replied. 'You ever thought of writing a self-help book?'

Caroline smiled. 'I can't even help myself half the time. I don't think I'm in any position to start helping other people. In any case, this is what we're in this job for, isn't it? We're here to solve people's issues and restore order and justice. That's got to be a form of therapy in itself.'

'Very true,' Dexter replied.

'Dex, listen to me. You're genuinely one of the best people I've ever worked with. If you feel threatened or worried for one moment that there's another DS on the team, I can tell you now you have nothing to worry about.'

Caroline saw Dexter's jaw tighten again.

'I don't feel threatened. I'm hardly gonna think my role is at risk because some jumped up little... Sorry. That bloke just pushes all my buttons.'

'It's alright. Honestly. Everyone's got buttons somewhere. It just turns out yours are very well hidden. And for good reason. They appear to be nuclear.'

Dexter let out a small chuckle, the thick atmosphere in the room disappearing by a solid half. 'Maybe it's a Caribbean thing. Laid-back and jovial, but God forgive you if you get on the wrong side.'

'A lovely sentiment for a lad born in Leicester.'

'Where they famously replace your entire genetic heritage with English DNA at the point of birth.'

Caroline smiled. 'Fair point. Just as long as you know I'll always consider you about as exotic as a bag of chips.'

'Well they're Belgian, so you're a little off with your geography, but it's a good start.'

Caroline looked at Dexter and smiled again. 'Good to have you back, Dex.'

Before he could reply, there was a knock at the door.

'Come in,' Caroline called, watching as Aidan entered the room. She recognised the eager look on his face immediately.

'Boss. I think we might have something,' he said.

23

Later that morning, Sara Henshaw was making herself a cup of tea in the station's kitchenette, her mind elsewhere as she enjoyed a moment's downtime.

'Great minds think alike,' Elijah Drummond said as he entered and walked over to the still-steaming kettle.

Sara let out a giggle, and immediately chastised herself. Coming across like a schoolgirl wasn't a good look, but she couldn't help herself.

'I bet you're a two sugars kind of girl, aren't you?' Elijah asked.

'One and a bit,' Sara replied, smiling.

'But two at heart, am I right?'

Her smile became a beam. 'I'm trying to cut down.'

'Aren't we all. You know, sometimes, doing this job I wonder why. Everyone's so worried about cutting sugar, reducing calories, drinking less. And then you come into work and pick up a file about a bloke in his twenties who's been stabbed in the street, or a woman killed by a hit and run driver at the age of thirty-five, and you wonder why you bother. If the Big Man's going to reach down and grab you sooner or later, you might as well enjoy a full-fat Coke in the meantime.'

'True,' Sara replied. 'But I'm pretty sure that body's not built on Big Macs and pork pies. Sorry. I didn't mean—'

'Hey, it's cool,' Elijah said, putting a hand on her shoulder. 'Don't apologise for a compliment. But you're right, babe. It's all about balance.'

Sara felt her heart jump. A part of her questioned whether it was appropriate for a more senior officer to call her "babe", but what was the harm? Would she have been more concerned if it was any other officer?

'Listen, there's something I wanted to ask you,' he continued. 'I hope I'm not stepping out of line here, but I wondered if perhaps you fancied going out for a drink after work one day?'

Sara stood, eyes wide, not quite sure what to say.

'Sorry, that was inappropriate of me. I meant just as a getting to know each other sort of thing. Team bonding, or whatever.'

'No, it's fine. It's just—'

'Ah. You've got a boyfriend, haven't you?'

'No. No, I haven't. I—'

'It's cool. Sorry, I shouldn't have said anything. I just... I mean, you're an incredibly attractive woman. And it might have just been me, but I thought I felt a spark when we were chatting in the office earlier.'

'It's not just you,' Sara said, finally managing to get the words out. 'I'd love to. It just came as a surprise, that's all. I didn't think for one second you'd be interested in me.'

Elijah cocked his head to one side and put his hand back on her shoulder. 'Sara, are you kidding me? Look at you. You're gorgeous. You're funny, you're bubbly. Why wouldn't any guy be interested? If anything, I wanted to make sure I got in there before anyone else did.'

Sara felt herself blushing, and chastised herself silently. It had been so long since anyone had shown an interest in her in this way, she could hardly remember when the last time was.

'You're very sweet,' she replied, getting a foothold over herself. 'But yes, I'd love to.'

'Great,' Elijah replied, beaming. 'I was thinking it might be best to avoid Oakham. Walls have ears, and all that. You know what people can be like when it comes to mixing things like this with work. Especially considering the whole rank thing. You know what I mean.'

'I know. I'd definitely give the Wheatsheaf a swerve, then,' Sara replied, laughing. 'That's practically our staff canteen.'

Elijah took his mobile phone from his suit pocket. 'Tell you what. Why don't you give me your number, and I'll have a think about where we could go and I'll text you. Saves any awkward clandestine conversations at work.'

'Yeah. That's a good idea,' Sara said, typing her number into Elijah's phone.

'Great. I'm really looking forward to it.'

'Me too.'

Before Sara had a chance to react, Elijah leant forward and kissed her on the cheek, before turning and heading back to the office. She stood, momentarily stunned, before letting out the breath she realised she'd been holding for far too long.

She glanced at the worktop in the kitchenette, noticing the mug of tea still sitting there.

'Elijah,' she called, not yet having noticed he was well out of earshot. 'You forgot your—'

24

Caroline rested her chin on the palm of her hand, her elbow propped on her desk.

'In any other case I'd say this was dynamite, but I think I'm even more confused now than I was before,' she said, having digested what Aidan had just told them. 'Thoughts, Dex?'

Dexter let out a breath. 'Christ. Yeah, I think I'd agree. It would explain why Susan Thornton was acting so strangely when we spoke to her. If she'd recently found out her husband was having an affair, you'd imagine there's a part of her that's pretty glad he's gone. But she barely said anything, and acted almost as if she just wanted to put the whole thing out of her mind and carry on. You don't think she was involved, do you?'

Caroline gave a mock shrug. 'Not my place to say. But without having had time to digest everything properly and look at it from a distance, my instinct would be that it was actually just very convenient timing for Susan. She doesn't strike me as the sort of woman to organise a hit on her husband. Especially when we already know the man we're looking for is connected with Norway in some way, with everything we know so far about his business dealings over there. It seems likely to me that's the answer here, and that Susan might feel she was done a favour by complete coincidence. If she even knew about the affair, that is.'

'We can easily find out,' Aidan offered. 'Are we doing coincidences now, then?'

A wry smile appeared on Caroline's face. She had to give him that one. 'Usually not, no. But they do happen. And when they do, they tend to be bigger than you might realise. I've seen some big cases get hampered and slowed down by detectives trying to find links where there aren't any. I find that if you feel yourself getting bogged down by that, apply Occam's razor.'

Aidan's blank reaction told Caroline she needed to offer an explanation. 'The simplest answer is often the right one,' she said. 'We humans tend to overthink things and look for convoluted patterns of logic. We try to make sense of every piece of information and link it all together without even realising what we're doing. Occam's razor says the simplest possible answer is usually the right one.'

'I'll take your word for it,' Aidan replied.

'Either way, we need to find out what Susan Thornton knew — if anything — and when. But tread carefully on that, because she might very well have known nothing. Her husband's just been killed, and if we wade in there, all guns blazing, firing off about how he'd been having an affair with another woman behind her back, it's hardly likely to help matters.'

'Do we know who the mystery woman is?' Dexter asked.

'Only that she's called Toni,' Aidan replied. 'Or at least, that's the name she's saved as in his phone. It's taken them up until now to get past the security on his phone. Honestly, it's best not to ask.'

Caroline looked back down at the sheets of paper on the desk in front of her — printouts of messages they'd obtained from Clive Thornton's phone. The earliest messages were only from the morning of Clive's murder, but they appeared to be a continuation of an existing conversation. Caroline considered this must mean Clive had been systematically deleting messages to and from Toni on a fairly regular basis, hiding the evidence trail.

[Toni 09:26] Sounds good to me! Looking forward to it ;-) xx

[Toni 12:21] How's your day going, sexy beast? Xx

[Toni 13:13] I'm guessing the joke about six coach loads of tourists came true!! :-P xx

[Toni 15:04] All messages left unread...? Hope everything's ok and you're just rushed off your feet. Or will Miss need to punish you later? Xx

[Toni 17:10] Are you ok? I thought maybe you might have left your phone at home but would've expected you to be back by now. Please let me know all's ok xx

[Toni 17:46] MISSED AUDIO CALL

[Toni 17:47] Clive, is everything ok? I'm getting worried now xx

[Toni 17:54] MISSED AUDIO CALL

[Toni 18:18] OK, I'm presuming this is something to do with what you said the other day about her finding out. I completely understand if you don't want to take the risk anymore. I can't pretend I'm not disappointed but of course I totally get it. It's not worth ruining your marriage over a bit of fun. It'd just be nice if you could let me know, so I know xx

[Toni 18:36] Clive, I'm guessing you've blocked my number or something. I'd rather you were able to just tell me it's over, but I get the hint. I don't know if this'll ever reach you or if you'll ever see it, but my door is always open. I really enjoyed our time together xx

'Where did we find Clive's phone?' Caroline asked. 'Was it on his person?'

'No, he'd left it at home that day,' Dexter replied. 'It was charging in his kitchen. His wife said he did forget it from time to time, but it had been a while since it'd happened. I guess some people just aren't as attached to their phones as others.'

'Very true. Not out of the ordinary, considering his generation. And Mrs Thornton was at home that day?'

'Yep.'

'So she might have seen messages flash up on the screen?'

'He had notification previews disabled. She would

have been able to see there *were* messages, but she wouldn't have been able to read them.'

'Would she have been able to see who they were from?'

'I'm not sure. But if so, it'd only show a name.'

'That'd be enough to get the red mist to descend, especially if she was already suspicious or had confronted him over it in the past,' Caroline said, immediately regretting the conspiratorial tone in her voice.

'True. And for all we know, she might know the PIN code to his phone. If she did, she'd have been able to read everything.'

Caroline nodded slowly. 'No wonder he didn't tend to leave his phone at home much anymore. Have we put in to the phone networks to find out who this Toni's number is registered to?'

'Yep, we're on it,' Aidan said.

'Good stuff. Once we've got an ID on her, we'll go and chat with her. I've a feeling that'll open up a whole lot more.'

Dexter's mobile phone rang in his pocket. Not recognising the number on the screen, he answered the call.

'Dexter Antoine.'

The voice at the other end of the phone was loud enough for everyone to hear.

'Hello, it's Andrea Ruston calling from Border Force, regarding your request for information on Mr Karlsen. Do you have a few moments? I've got something that might be of interest to you.'

25

Dexter ended the call and put his phone back in his pocket, having jotted some notes down on a scrap of paper during the call.

'Okay, that was Border Force,' he said to the others, as if they hadn't overheard. 'They've got a record of Karlsen entering the UK at Stansted Airport around midday on Friday the sixteenth, and leaving Heathrow on the evening of Monday the nineteenth. They confirmed he flew in on a Norwegian passport in the name of Oyvind Andreas Karlsen. There was a Ryanair flight in from Oslo Gardermoen around that time on Friday, and a British Airways one back to the same airport from Heathrow on Monday night. We'd have to check with the airlines, but it's highly likely they're the flights he was on.'

'What are the times of those flights?' Caroline asked.

'The flight from Oslo on Friday arrived just before midday, and the one back on Monday was scheduled for five-past-eight in the evening, but took off about half an hour late.'

'Five-past-eight, Heathrow,' Caroline muttered, doing some mental maths. 'What's that, about two hours by road?'

'At least,' Aidan replied. 'Even if he left Oakham immediately after killing Clive Thornton, he'd be hitting the Black Cat Roundabout at about five, half-five, and that's always snarled up in rush hour. Going down past Northampton and Milton Keynes won't have been much better, either. In any case, you're looking at reaching the M25 at six-ish, maybe half-six. I can't imagine that'll have been flowing freely a few days before Christmas.'

'Okay,' Caroline said, nodding slowly. 'So even with a best case scenario, assuming he kills Clive within seconds of the castle closing, then hotfoots it down to Heathrow and somehow dodges all the traffic, he'd arrive shortly after six o'clock. That's doable for an eight o'clock flight, especially if he only had hand luggage. If you add in the likely traffic, though, we're probably looking at, what, three hours? That gets him to Heathrow around seven, even if he left Oakham immediately. I can't imagine trains or public transport would have been any quicker. Again, probably just about doable if he only had hand luggage, but he'd be cutting it pretty damn close. Heathrow would've been heaving with people flying home for Christmas.'

'True,' Dexter replied. 'But at the same time, he wouldn't have wanted to be hanging around in the UK for any longer than necessary, especially after what'd just happened.'

Caroline had an uneasy feeling. 'I don't know. It feels even riskier. If he missed his flight, which he had a good chance of doing, he'd have been stuck here til the next morning. He'd have had no way of knowing until it was too late. What are Karlsen's last known movements from CCTV?'

Aidan flicked back a couple of pages in his notebook. 'At three o'clock on Monday, he comes into the castle and takes photos of the horseshoes. He's there just over a minute before leaving again. We don't know where he goes after that, but he's not picked up on CCTV in the town or the market square. If he left through the main gate, you'd expect to see him. That means it's likely he headed across the castle grounds and up and over the steps towards the Burley Road car park. I think it'd be worth checking the reg numbers of the vehicles parked there that day and cross-referencing them with ANPR in the vicinity of the airports.'

'Either that or he was hiding out somewhere, waiting for the castle to close. It would have been easy enough for him to find his way back in through a side door that's not covered by CCTV. But there's nothing on the town and council cameras after four o'clock either?'

'No, not that we can find. Although you'd expect he'd have scoped out where the cameras were and would be deliberately avoiding them where possible.'

'Except for having walked bold as brass, right into the

Great Hall of the castle on two separate occasions, knowing he'd be picked up on all of them.'

'But there's no way he could be identified from those images,' Aidan replied. 'That's why he wore the hat and kept his head low.'

'And then wrote his name in the visitors' book.'

'A name we presume to be false. If this really is some sort of government-backed spy operation, it wouldn't matter if he wrote the fake name that's in his passport, because any requests we put in to the Norwegian authorities would be brushed aside.'

'I don't know,' Caroline said, shaking her head. 'The diplomatic fallout would be insane. And if they were really that casual about leaving traces, why bother with the hat? Something just isn't adding up here. What do you think, Dex?' she asked, noticing her colleague had kept silent while she spoke.

'Honestly? I dunno. I think the best thing we can do is wait to hear from the Norwegian police. If they're cooperative, we'll be able to get all the information we need about Karlsen. If they're uncooperative? Well... That'll tell us even more.'

26

Having obtained the phone number of Toni — Clive Thornton's apparent lover — from Clive's mobile, it hadn't taken long for them to track down her full identity through her mobile phone network.

Dexter had arranged to visit the woman they now knew as Antonia Scott at her home in Oakham. At first, Caroline had been hesitant about accepting Dexter's request to accompany him, being hyper-aware of her need to take a back seat and allow him to come into his own. She was a sucker for a compliment, though. It only took Dexter to point out how much better than him she was at decoding body language and spotting when something wasn't quite right with someone's story, before she found herself in the car with him, on the way to Antonia Scott's home.

It was a beautiful light-coloured house, constructed in the local limestone, and it yet again struck Caroline how rare it was to find an ugly building in Rutland — especially when compared to most other places.

They parked in front of the double garage, and made their way across the gravel driveway to the front door. A few moments after Dexter had administered his policeman's knock, a woman came to the door. She seemed to be around fifty, and although she clearly wasn't someone who tried to hide her age, her calm confidence in her own skin gave her a certain youthful innocence.

'Mrs Scott?' Dexter asked.

'Yes?'

'I'm Detective Sergeant Dexter Antoine from Rutland Police, and this is my colleague, Detective Inspector Caroline Hills. Can we come in please?'

Dexter saw the familiar panic in Toni's eyes. 'Why? What's happened? Is something wrong?'

'If we can come in, we'll be able to explain everything right away.'

Toni stepped aside, and Caroline and Dexter walked in, heading straight for the living room. They sat down on one of the sofas, silently inviting Toni to do the same.

'Mrs Scott, I—'

'Please. Call me Toni.'

'Okay,' Dexter replied. 'Toni, I'm afraid we have some bad news. A body has been discovered locally. It's been identified as that of Clive Thornton, who we believe you knew.'

It always felt like delivering a hammer blow, but the training had been clear: don't prevaricate, don't stall —

get straight to the point and leave no room for misinterpretation.

Toni seemed to freeze for a moment, before a range of micro-expressions crossed her face as the news slowly sank in.

'He's dead?' she croaked eventually.

'I'm afraid so. I realise it must come as quite a shock, but we do need to ask you some important questions. Can you tell me how you knew Clive?'

Toni took a moment to compose herself before speaking. 'I don't really know what to say,' she answered, her voice almost a whisper. 'Do you want to know how we met? What happened to him? I mean... How?'

'We'll go into that in a short while, I promise. For now we just need to get some more information. How would you describe your relationship with him?'

Toni looked to the ceiling and slowly shook her head. 'I think that's probably the one question I can't answer. He's been getting more and more distant over the last week or so. You probably already know this, but Clive's married. I was just his... I don't know. His release. He told me last week that he thought his wife had found out about us. Said she'd been acting strangely. He kind of pulled back a bit at that point, and I got the impression he thought maybe it wasn't worth the risk.'

'Risking his marriage, you mean?' Dexter asked, having sensed that Caroline had picked up on the same thing he had.

'Yes. Risking everything. Clive does a lot of good.

Charity work, things like that. They've got children. Grown up ones, but still. It's the sort of thing that can ruin a family if it gets out.'

'And have you ever met his wife?'

'No. No, but Clive told me quite a bit about her.'

'Like what?'

'Nothing that'll be of any use to you, I'm sure. Just that she preferred to play the dutiful housewife, burying her head in the sand and getting on with things rather than wanting to rock the boat. My sense was that Clive wanted to put a stop to things with me and allow her to keep that boat steady before it tipped over.'

'And did he say what might happen if it did tip over?' Dexter asked.

'Oh no, I didn't mean like that. She doesn't get angry or anything. Not from what Clive was saying. I just mean that everyone's got a stage where they say "enough is enough", haven't they? And maybe he sensed she was getting close to that stage, so he wanted to pull the plug on what we had in order to save his marriage.'

'And how did that make you feel?'

Toni thought for a moment before giving a slight shrug. 'It is what it is, isn't it? Mine and Clive's relationship was a casual one, to say the least. It's not like there was any danger of us falling in love and getting married or anything.'

'And when you say casual...'

'I mean sex.'

Dexter looked down at his notebook and feigned scribbling. 'Right. Yes. Alright. Okay.'

'Clive has a side to him that doesn't receive attention within his marriage. That's not to say his relationship with his wife is sexless, but he has... He likes some other aspects.'

As much as he didn't want to, Dexter knew he was going to have to ask.

'Such as?' he croaked.

Toni took a deep breath. 'Sometimes, men — or women — who are used to spending their lives being a leader or the person in charge all the time... Well, they like to experience the opposite in their downtime. They like to be submissive, particularly in a sexual sense.'

Dexter paused for a moment. 'Okay.'

'It's a release. A chance to be someone else, or at least play a different psychological role. If you're used to being in control, being able to explore the feeling of someone else being in control can be extremely liberating.'

'Okay. Right. And... I mean, what sort of...'

'Are you sure you want to hear this?' Toni asked.

'I'm a man of the world, Mrs Scott,' Dexter replied.

Toni gave a small smile. 'Trust me, the world's bigger than you think it is. Clive liked to be tied up. Blindfolded. Gagged. Completely at the mercy of whatever I wanted to do to him.'

'And what would... You know.'

'Whatever I fancied at the time. Whipping, beating,

tickling, teasing. I know what you're thinking. Probably the same as most people think. But everything had been spoken about at great length long before we ever did anything. We were both well aware of each other's boundaries, and ultimately Clive was able to say no at any time he liked.'

'But if he was gagged...'

'We had a system. Safety and consent are everything. What a lot of people don't understand is that the dominant — that's me — isn't the one in control at all. Ultimately, it's the submissive who has the power to put a stop to everything immediately, and who willingly puts themself into that situation. They set the rules, the boundaries, everything. Then, within that framework, they can completely let go. It's a bit like going on a rollercoaster. You do it because the track and the ride have been safety checked and designed to be completely safe. You pay good money to go on it. You pull the safety bar down, knowing you're secure and then you're able to let go and enjoy the feeling of freefall in absolutely safety. It's the exact same feeling you'd get from driving your car off the edge of a cliff, but I think given the choice most people would prefer a rollercoaster. You get to enjoy those "unpleasant" feelings, for want of a better word, in a safe space without any of the risk that's usually associated with it.'

'Okay,' Dexter replied. 'Well, I've got to say, I've definitely learnt something today. And you were Clive's rollercoaster, were you?'

'I guess that'd be one way of putting it, yes. These sorts of relationships can be pretty turbulent, anyway.'

The conversation stopped as they heard footsteps coming down the stairs, shortly followed by the living room door opening.

'Hello darling,' Toni said, addressing a woman of about thirty. 'This is my daughter, Kelly.'

'Hi Kelly,' Dexter said, smiling.

'Hi,' came the response.

'Do you want to wait upstairs? I'll be up shortly. We just need to have a little chat down here.'

'Okay,' Kelly replied, before turning to head back upstairs.

'If you think of anything that might help, I'll leave a card with your mum,' Dexter called.

Kelly looked back and nodded, before rounding the corner back into the hall and disappearing from sight.

Caroline raised her eyebrow to Dexter, which thankfully went unnoticed by Kelly's mum.

'She's thirty-three,' Toni said, without being asked. 'She has what used to be known as Asperger's Syndrome. She's very quiet. Likes a lot of her own time. Do you need to speak to her? Only, with her condition being as it is, it can be tricky sometimes.'

'I think we should be okay for now,' Dexter replied, giving a smile.

'Oh god, I'm so sorry. I didn't even offer you a cup of tea or coffee,' Toni said, rising to her feet. 'What would you like?'

'A glass of water would be fine, thanks,' Dexter said.

'Coffee, please,' Caroline replied. 'Black, no sugar.'

'No worries. Back in a tick.'

A few moments after Toni left the room, Dexter leaned in towards Caroline.

'Bit weird the wife never mentioned all this, isn't it? Especially if she'd recently found out.'

'We don't know for sure that she did. Only that Clive suspected she'd found out. But you're right — it stood out like a sore thumb for me, too. Especially when you think about how strangely she'd been acting the whole time we were round there.'

Dexter's mobile phone started to ring, vibrating in the pocket of his suit jacket.

He took the phone out and glanced at the screen. The caller's number began with +47, and Dexter knew instantly what this meant.

'Dexter Antoine,' he said, answering the call.

'Detective Sergeant Antoine, this is Camilla Svendsen calling from the National Police Directorate in Oslo. How are you?'

'I'm fine thanks, Camilla. And yourself?'

'I'm very good, thank you. Only a few hours to go until my Christmas break begins. And I'm very pleased to give you a little Christmas present. We have located Oyvind Andreas Karlsen. I understand you wish to speak with him in connection with a murder inquiry, is this correct?'

'Yes, that's right,' Dexter replied.

'Okay. Are you looking to make an arrest at this time? I don't think we have a record of a mutual legal assistance request here.'

'No, we haven't submitted an MLA. At the moment we're keen to speak to Mr Karlsen and hopefully eliminate him from our investigation.'

'I see. Of course, without an MLA request we cannot guarantee anything, but I can tell you he does not have any previous convictions here in Norway. He appears to work as a doctor in the city of Sandefjord, which is approximately one hundred and twenty kilometres from Oslo.'

'Okay. And what are our options, Camilla? How can we speak with Mr Karlsen?'

'Well, if you wanted to make a formal arrest then an MLA would be required. But I have to tell you it might be difficult over the Christmas period. Our staffing here is a little... relaxed... at the moment. The alternative is to request a voluntary interview with him. We can facilitate that if you wish, but of course he would not be obliged to do so if that is what he decides.'

Dexter considered this for a moment. Was their evidence on Karlsen strong enough to go through formal diplomatic channels in order to have him arrested and potentially extradited? As things stood, no matter how suspicious and damning it might seem, the evidence on paper was entirely circumstantial.

'How would the voluntary interview process work?' he asked her.

'Typically, we would either call him or visit him at home and explain that the police in the United Kingdom wished to speak with him about an investigation. If he chose to cooperate and to speak with you, we would arrange for him to attend a local police station, where you would be able to meet him and ask any questions you need for your investigation. Of course, this would be done under the supervision of an officer from the National Police Directorate.'

'In Norway?'

'Yes, I am afraid we do not have any Norwegian police stations in the UK at this moment,' Camilla replied, her deadpan manner making Dexter smile.

'Worth a shot,' he said. 'Okay. Leave it with me. Can I call you back on this number?'

'Sure. Speak to you soon.'

'Great. Thanks. Bye.'

Having ended the call, Dexter looked at his phone for a moment, before looking up at Caroline.

'Don't suppose you know where your passport is, do you?' he asked.

27

Back in Rutland later that evening, Sara Henshaw's heart jumped as the door opened and Elijah Drummond walked into The Fox at North Luffenham, before joining her at a quiet table in the corner.

The log-burning stove was roaring away, throwing out more than enough heat to keep the cold December chill at bay.

'Sorry I'm a bit late,' Elijah said. 'Do you want another drink?'

'If you're sure,' Sara replied, noticing that even though she'd only been there a few minutes herself, she'd almost finished her first Bacardi and Coke.

Once he'd bought the drinks, Elijah settled himself into the wingback chair and took a sip of his beer.

'I presume you're not driving, then?' he said, nodding towards her two drinks glasses.

'Ah. No, I decided to get a taxi in the end. You were right — it's easier. Plus I think I needed the Dutch courage.'

Elijah smiled. 'Nothing to be nervous about. It's not like you don't know me. Besides which, it's not like we can get to know each other much better at work, is it?'

Sara returned his smile. 'It can be a bit full-on at times. I imagine it's a pretty different atmosphere to what you're used to.'

'Oh god, just a bit. I can see why Hills is so keen to keep as much as she can on a local level. Just trying to bring all the processes and procedures into line with EMSOU would be a nightmare. It's taking a bit of getting used to, but I actually quite like it. It's a lot more relaxed.'

Sara laughed. 'Wow. I dread to think what counts as full-on at EMSOU, then.'

'I think it's probably a different type of full-on. Find me a policing job anywhere in the country where there's not always a pile of things to do. I think it's just the general atmosphere here that's different. Everyone seems to know everyone, it's less frenetic and there's not so much pen pushing. It's definitely not a bad thing.'

Sara shrugged. 'I guess it's what I'm used to. It's all I've ever known, really. I've not worked for another force.'

'I wouldn't recommend it. You've got a really good number here, I can tell you. There's definitely nothing to be gained in the bigger forces. Not unless you're one of those ladder climbers.'

'I think you can probably tell I'm not.'

'I did get that impression,' Elijah said, smiling.

Sara looked at him for a few moments, then picked up her drink and took a couple of sips as she looked around the pub. She didn't want to come across as weird or too keen. That had put men off before. She needed to answer one simple question: was she keen on Elijah Drummond because she genuinely liked him, or was it because he was a man who'd showed her the slightest bit of attention? She'd fallen for the latter too many times in the past, and it had never worked out well. The trouble was, it was difficult to work out one from the other.

If she was completely honest with herself, she wondered if this time there might be a third option: that this was merely a way of getting over Aidan and trying to forget how keen she'd been on him. And although that might have been a necessary step, Sara knew it wouldn't be a healthy one.

'It's been ages since I've been out,' Elijah said, jolting her from her thoughts.

'Oh?'

'Been too wrapped up in work, I guess. And not really had anyone to go out with. But I've got to say, I'm really enjoying your company.'

Sara smiled at him. She couldn't lie — it felt great to be appreciated.

'I've not been out much either,' she replied. 'A few drinks with the team after work from time to time, but that's about it.'

'No dates?' Elijah asked.

'No. Not really.'

'Not really?'

Sara sighed. 'Well, there was someone at work I was kind of into, but it never went anywhere. I'll be honest, sometimes I wonder if I still might be. But as I say, it never went anywhere.'

'Someone on the team?'

Sara chuckled. 'I can't answer that. If I said yes, it'd narrow it down to two guys.'

'Dexter?'

'No. No, not Dexter.'

'Blimey. Then that only leaves Adrian.'

'Aidan.'

'Does he know you're keen? Or were.'

'No. He's got a girlfriend.'

Elijah nodded slowly. 'Ah. In that case it's probably best not to say anything. Trust me, I've been in that position before and it doesn't end well. Has he been with her long?'

'Not really, no. A few months.'

'I hate to say it, but if he was single before that and he knew you were single... Well, if he was interested he would've made a move, wouldn't he?'

Sara swallowed hard. This was more or less the conclusion she'd come to at the time, but it was the first time she'd heard it voiced. In a way, she knew it was something she needed to hear from someone else.

'I know,' she replied. 'Like I said, it never went anywhere.'

'Sorry. I didn't mean to sound harsh. Honestly, I sympathise completely. I've been there, and it's horrible. I hope I didn't upset you.'

'No, not at all. You were right. It was all a bit silly, really. I guess I had this kind of tunnel vision, where I was focused so much on Aidan and whether to tell him how I felt, time just passed me by. The longer it went on, the harder it got. If I'd just been upfront with him right away, I would've had an answer. But I was scared of what the answer might have been. It's stupid, because if it had been a no, I could've just moved on and that would've been that. But I didn't. I kept it to myself, it kept growing, and by the time I was on the verge of doing something about it, he'd met Keira. And who knows what opportunities I missed in the meantime?'

Elijah gave a sympathetic smile. 'You can't look at it that way. What's done is done. You can't change the past. I guess all you can do is learn from it and make sure you don't pass up those opportunities in the future.'

'Yeah. True.'

'Or the present.'

Sara looked at him. Now she knew this wasn't just a man showing her the slightest bit of attention. He was clearly very keen on her. Whilst part of her screamed "why?!" another was pushing it down and telling her not to self-sabotage yet again. Was she as keen on him? Instinctively, she thought so. He was her type: dark hair, nice eyes, a strong jaw. Confident, but sensitive.

As Elijah leaned in towards her, she closed her eyes

and settled her internal dilemma with three words: What's the harm?

28

Just before 9.30pm local time, Caroline and Dexter's plane touched down at Torp Sandefjord Airport. Their onward journey into Sandefjord itself would take them less than fifteen minutes, and the pair had made a note to ask Karlsen why he'd instead chosen to fly in and out of Oslo Gardermoen — a two-hour drive away, on the other side of Norway's capital city.

They were due to speak to Karlsen first thing in the morning, and were hoping to catch the 2pm flight back home. Having checked in advance, there were still plenty of seats available on both that departure and the late evening one, so they'd opted to play it by ear and book the return flight at the last minute. They didn't want to spend any longer in Norway than they had to, but at the same time they didn't want to rush the time they had with Karlsen.

After they'd checked into their rooms at the Hotel

Kong Carl, they headed down to the hotel's restaurant for a late dinner and a nightcap.

'Feels strange being away so close to Christmas,' Caroline said, trying to draw Dexter into conversation. He'd been unusually quiet throughout their journey, and she'd wondered if perhaps he was a nervous traveller. Now they had arrived and checked in, she'd expected him to have brightened up. 'You must be glad to be getting away from Elijah Drummond for a day or so, at least.'

'I was tempted to send him instead of me,' Dexter replied. 'But it didn't seem like a good idea.'

Caroline smiled. 'Probably for the best. He needs to be brought a little more up to speed before he gets to enjoy the perks.'

'No, I mean I wouldn't be able to stop myself cancelling his return ticket.'

Caroline laughed. 'I'd be willing to put money on the two of you being best buds by Easter. It's always the way with these things.'

'I wouldn't count on it,' Dexter replied. 'If he's still here at Easter, I won't be.'

'Give him time. He'll settle down. It's a very different culture here to EMSOU. It took me a while coming from the Met. It just takes a little adjustment. Or a lot of it, in his case.'

The waiter arrived at their table, and they placed their order for dinner, choosing to pay for their drinks separately. There was no way they'd be reimbursed by work for alcohol, but what they didn't know wouldn't hurt them.

'You got any plans for Christmas?' Caroline asked Dexter, as they demolished the complimentary basket of bread rolls.

'Nah, not really. I'm going over to my parents'. My brother and his missus will be there too. Usual fare. You?'

'Quiet one at home. It's the first Christmas without Mark's parents, so he's not keen on going all-out. Something a bit more muted, I think. You got all your presents bought?'

'Not yet,' Dexter replied, looking at the table and blinking a few times. 'I'll have to do a last-minute shopping run when we get back.'

'Amazon's your friend now, Dex. Take full advantage of next-day delivery. You don't want to be traipsing round the shops this week. You could order it all now and it'd be waiting for you when you get back.'

Dexter nodded. 'Yeah. True.'

'Something else on your mind?' Caroline asked, after they'd sat in silence for almost another full minute.

'How do you mean?' Dexter replied.

'Just in general. You've seemed a bit flat this week. Not quite your usual self.'

Dexter gave a shrug. 'I'm just knackered, I suppose. Short days and long dark nights. Trying to get Christmas stuff sorted. You know how it is.'

'We can't all smile all the time, eh?' Caroline replied.

'How you feeling about work? Apart from the Drummond thing, I mean.'

'Yeah, fine. No probs there.'

'Feels like a lot of pressure heading up your first murder case, doesn't it? I remember it well. It's like you're the only one in the world who's responsible for that person's legacy, not to mention justice for the family. But no matter whose name's on the front of the file, we're still the same team. We'll still get the same results. You know how hard I find it to step back and not get too involved in things. It's bloody impossible. I've never been able to do it. But not for one second have I had a single doubt or second thought about letting you run the show. And I think that says a lot.'

'Yeah,' Dexter replied, his voice quiet. 'Yeah, I'm not worried about any of that. It's good to be able to step up and get that experience. I really appreciate it.'

Caroline looked at him for a few moments. 'What's up then, Dex? You can tell me. I know we're work colleagues and whatever, but I can also be a friend. I consider all of you my friends. You've all given me a lot without even knowing it. You especially.'

Dexter seemed to think about this for a short while. She could tell there was something playing on his mind, and it must be something big. He wasn't the sort of person to let things bother him — especially not small things. Whatever it was, he was clearly uncomfortable with the prospect of telling her. Her only assumption was that it must be work-related. Otherwise, why wouldn't he want to open up?

'Honestly, it's nothing,' Dexter said, eventually.

'It?' Caroline replied. 'If it's an it, it must be something. But listen, if you don't want to tell me, that's fine. Whenever you're ready, I'm here, alright?'

Dexter didn't respond. He seemed to still be deep in thought.

A few moments later, he opened his mouth to speak, his words quiet and stuttering.

'The thing is... I just... The other day... I...'

Before Dexter could form a complete sentence, the waiter arrived with their meals. Despite the basket of bread rolls, they were both still hungrier than they'd been in a long time. As the minutes passed and the food on their plates began to disappear, so too did the memory of their conversation.

29

The police station in Sandefjord looked reassuringly like a police station in any British town or city. The familiar red brick building with its high brown windows gave Caroline and Dexter the comfort of familiarity as they arrived for their interview with Karlsen.

They'd rightly — and correctly — expected the Norwegian police to have an officer in attendance, but they were surprised at the addition of an interpreter, having discovered so far that most Norwegian people spoke better English than they did.

That distinction applied equally to Karlsen. Even though they'd spent barely a minute or so in Karlsen's company, there was no doubting the interpreter was picking up a nice little Christmas bonus for no reason whatsoever.

Karlsen appeared to be an amiable sort of fellow, if a little nervous and confused.

'I don't know how much you've been told about why we're here, Mr Karlsen,' Dexter said, 'but we wanted to speak with you about an incident that happened in Oakham, Rutland, earlier this week. We believe you were visiting the area, is that correct?'

'Yes, that's right.'

'Why was that?'

Karlsen seemed even more confused at this question. 'I visit the UK regularly. I have friends in the area, and I'm interested in the history.'

'And you had two nights in Oakham, is that correct?'

'Yes, that's right.'

'Did you stay with friends?'

'No, I stayed in a hotel. This time I came only to explore Rutland and the history. I had a few days of vacation from work, and I wanted to use them.'

'Do you live alone here?'

'Yes. I was married, but now I'm divorced and I live alone. I try to use my spare time travelling or doing things I want to do. Because now I can.'

Dexter smiled reflexively. 'I don't blame you,' he said.

Beside him, Caroline was leafing through some documentation the Norwegian police had provided, comparing them with her own notes on Karlsen. It didn't take her long before a heavy realisation began to dawn. She looked again at the documents in front of her, and again at her notes.

'Oh no,' she whispered quietly to herself, pleased no-one else had heard.

She waited for a gap in the conversation, then gently placed a hand on Dexter's arm.

'DS Antoine, could I have a quick moment with you outside the room please?'

30

'Did the Norwegian police send any documentation to you via email at all?' Caroline asked Dexter as they stood in the corridor outside the interview room at Sandefjord police station.

'I don't think so. It was all done over the phone. Why's that?'

'Look at his name,' Caroline replied, showing her one of the documents she'd been reading a few moments ago.

'What about it? Am I missing something?'

'Øyvind Andreas Karlsen, Dex. With a line through the O on Øyvind. He didn't cross out his name in the visitors book at the castle. The O with a line through it is his first initial. It's a Norwegian O.'

Dexter closed his eyes as Caroline watched his shoulders slump.

'Jesus Christ,' he whispered, before taking a couple of

steps further down the corridor away from her. A few moments later, he turned round. 'But that doesn't mean he's got nothing to do with the murder.'

'True, but it's a pretty big mark of suspicion that no longer exists. Apart from looking a bit odd, the only reason we took an interest in him was the assumption that Andreas Karlsen was a pseudonym.'

Dexter shook his head. 'It still doesn't explain everything. In fact, I don't think it explains anything.'

'It makes him far less suspicious,' Caroline replied.

'I'm not sure it does. It just leaves another question unanswered. The answer might still be that he's guilty as anything. It doesn't mean everything else no longer fits. It does.'

'Not enough to chase it, Dex.'

'I'm not chasing,' Dexter replied, with more volume than was usual for him. Spotting Caroline's raised eyebrows, he repeated himself more quietly. 'I'm not chasing. I just don't think this lets him off the hook. So he wrote his real name. And what? We're still presuming that *is* his real name, by the way, and that the Norwegian authorities haven't kept up the charade by allowing us to come over here and ask questions to a guy, keeping us under the illusion that *is* his name. Whether he has an O before his name or not, and whether he draws a line through it or not, doesn't make it any more or less real.'

'And if he hadn't drawn a line through it, would we still have flown to Norway to speak to him?' Caroline asked.

Dexter was silent. That told them both everything they needed to know.

31

As Caroline walked into work the next morning, it felt almost as if her brief trip to Norway had never happened. It was more like an uncomfortable dream than anything. That feeling didn't last long, though, as she acknowledged her expected summons to Chief Superintendent Derek Arnold's office.

She'd always found Arnold to be firm but fair — a man who liked to keep an eye on things, but appreciated that Caroline's unconventional approach tended to yield results. And as far as he and his role were concerned, results were what mattered most. Today, though, there was no sign of amiability on Arnold's face. This was a man who looked thoroughly peed off.

'Sit down, Caroline,' he said, barely able to look at her. 'I think you've probably got a fair idea as to why I called you in here.'

Caroline said nothing for a moment or two while she tried to choose the right words. 'Yes,' she said eventually. 'And I can completely see how it looks from where you're sitting. But I'd appreciate the chance to explain things from my perspective, if I may, sir.'

'I'd very much like it if you did,' Arnold replied, leaning back in his chair and crossing his arms.

'As you know, in the process of reviewing CCTV footage from the castle, we discovered a man who'd visited the castle twice and who we considered to have been acting suspiciously. Crucially, the second time he visited the castle was just a couple of hours before Clive Thornton was murdered. Through the castle's guestbook, we discovered his identity and made some enquiries. It turns out he was from Norway. Around the same time, we also discovered Clive Thornton had been involved in a potential hydropower contract in Norway, which had been worth a huge sum of money but had subsequently fallen through. We felt we had reason to believe Karlsen, the Norwegian, might have been in the country under an assumed identity, and we were exploring the possibility that these aspects might have been linked and would provide an explanation for what happened to Clive Thornton.'

'When you say you had reason to believe Karlsen was here under an assumed identity, you mean you'd jumped to the conclusion this was some sort of Scandinavian James Bond conspiracy theory, long before you'd even thought to check the Norwegian alphabet.'

'That was a regrettable oversight, sir, but even if we had spotted it, it wouldn't have automatically taken Karlsen out of the frame.'

'No, but it would have saved a precious chunk of the operational budget, which you instead chose to waste on flights and hotels. An operational budget which, let me remind you, is extremely stretched as it is.'

Caroline clenched her teeth. It had been Arnold who had suggested she and Dexter visit Karlsen in Norway. He either had a very short memory, or he was deliberately trying to dodge responsibility. Either way, Caroline knew it would do her no good to argue back.

'I understand, sir. And I can only apologise.'

Arnold let out a harrumph. 'Apologies don't change budgets, Caroline. I can tell you I speak from experience on that one. You've wasted resources, you've wasted time, and you've risked public embarrassment. We're extremely lucky this story hasn't leaked out into the press as it is. How do you think they'd handle this little twist in the tale?'

Caroline knew the level of public hysteria that occurred when even the smallest inconvenience happened locally. She was sure the good people of Rutland wouldn't react well to discovering they'd not only managed to keep a local murder from the press, but that they'd wasted public money on a pointless trip to Norway.

She accepted there might come a point where she'd need to appeal for eyewitnesses or anyone who had information that could help. That was a possibility in all murder cases. But where they were confident of getting a result without that assistance, there were a lot of benefits to letting sleeping dogs lie. Public awareness was not always a good thing, and on occasion it could even muddy the waters further.

'Sir, I can't change what's already happened,' she said, addressing the Chief Superintendent's question and ignoring her building rage at his shirking of responsibility. 'It was a misjudgement. In any case, even though we've ascertained that Karlsen probably wasn't using a pseudonym, it doesn't mean he wasn't involved. There are further links we're looking into, and between you and me, I expect we'll find more. From where I am, something isn't quite sitting right.'

'Must be all that pickled herring you ate on your little trip away. I don't suppose I need to remind you that I've already had to bust a gut to have additional funding allocated to your department? You've only had your new lad with you a matter of days. We can't afford to waste another penny. How's he getting on?'

Caroline felt her eyebrows rise and her breathing stop as she tried to think of a diplomatic way to word her response.

'Uh, well it's still early days,' she said eventually.

'Every day counts, Caroline. You don't need me to tell you that. I need you to focus on getting him up to speed immediately. Yesterday. It's a hell of a time to be adding a new member to the team, right in the middle of an investigation.'

Caroline bit her tongue. She'd been asking Arnold for

months to come good on his promise of an extra team member, and it was only after Operation Titan had got into full swing that he'd finally delivered.

'Yes, sir,' she said, gritting her teeth. 'I'll keep you updated.'

32

By the time Caroline got back to the incident room, Dexter had already launched into his morning briefing.

She stepped into the room quietly and made her way to the back, where she perched on a desk as she watched him in action.

'In short,' he said, 'we're certainly not discounting Karlsen. There are still links we need to explain. But I think we need to cast our net wider. There are a few things which still aren't quite falling into place. The interview with Toni Scott didn't reveal a huge amount, but we think there's more to be had there. Even if she and Clive weren't life partners, she definitely knew a lot about his psychological makeup. That might give us a key that unlocks a new door somewhere along the line. Don't forget, we can always discount information that isn't relevant. But we can't do that if we don't find it in the first place, and even worse, we won't find the stuff that *is* relevant. So let's make sure we scoop the lot up, then get sieving. Any questions at this stage?'

Elijah Drummond put his hand up.

'Elijah.'

'Should we use a colander first, to drain all the big bits before we move onto a sieve?'

Dexter detected the slightest hint of a chuckle from Sara.

'No, I'm not sure that's necessary. Or funny. There are three angles I'd like us to look at primarily,' he said, returning to the rest of the team. 'The first is the break-in at the Thorntons' house. What spooked the intruders? Why didn't they take anything? Why didn't Susan Thornton want more to be done? It doesn't fit with the usual pattern of victims of break-ins, even if nothing was taken. It does happen, but it's not common, so I think bearing everything else in mind it's worth looking into further. The second is the Norwegian hydroelectric deal Clive was working on. We need to find out what exactly went wrong, what the consequences were, who lost out and who blamed Clive for that happening. Is it a big enough motive? Was there any point in wanting him dead? Thirdly, I think it's worth looking into Clive's charity links. We know he was actively involved in fundraising and voluntary work during his career, and remained so in retirement. Charities can be complicated pieces of machinery, and there are large sums of money floating around, not to mention a lot of people trying to do the right thing by vulnerable people. That could be ripe for some form of wrongdoing that'd lead to a motive for murder. And yes, I'm aware I'm speculating here, but we don't have a whole lot else to go on right now. We need to get our heads down and crack on with this.'

Dexter watched as Elijah leaned over to Sara and murmured — just loudly enough for him to hear, 'Oh, I was hoping to go home and have the day off, actually.'

Dexter rolled his tongue around in his mouth as he felt his blood pressure rising. Whichever way he turned, whatever he did or said, Elijah Drummond was getting right on his tits.

33

A few minutes after the morning briefing ended, Caroline invited Elijah into her office for a quick word. Although Operation Titan was officially Dexter's, he and Elijah Drummond were both Detective Sergeants, and Caroline had detected a friendly warning from Dexter might not go down quite as well as a word from a senior officer. She'd detected Elijah's lack of respect for Dexter early on in his secondment, and she felt that now was the time to nip it in the bud — in the most official way possible.

'Ma'am,' Elijah said as he entered the office and closed the door behind him.

'Don't worry, I won't keep you long,' Caroline said as she rounded her desk and sat down behind it. 'I just wanted a quick word, as I've noticed there have been one or two comments and moments that haven't gone down well over the past few days.'

'Sorry, ma'am. What sort of comments and moments?'

Elijah asked, as if this was the first time he'd ever heard either of those two words.

'For one, the comment you made towards the end of DS Antoine's morning briefing a short while ago,' she replied, her voice a little louder and more forceful than before. 'I was standing right behind you, and I could see full well that DS Antoine heard it from the front of the room as well. Off the back of your snarky comment about sieves and colanders, I thought someone should break it to you that it didn't exactly go down well.'

Caroline locked eyes with Elijah. His brash nature was quickly disappearing, and seemed to be replaced by a look of real shock and worry.

'I mean... I didn't mean anything by it,' he said, his voice stumbling. 'I guess I was just trying to inject a bit of humour, bring the team together a little bit, maybe.'

'The team is just fine together, Elijah. We're a tight-knit bunch. We've been working closely with each other for quite some time. You can't just waltz in and start making sarcastic remarks about colleagues and expect that everyone's going to start laughing at the expense of someone they've spent almost every waking hour with for the last however many years. That's not how it works.'

Elijah looked down at the desk, then back up at Caroline. 'I'm sorry, ma'am. Maybe it's just taking me a bit of getting used to. We don't have that sort of closeness at EMSOU. I mean, there are people you work with closely, or colleagues who've been on a few jobs together, but not like this. Not where it's the same team on each job. It's a finely tuned machine, I can see that.'

'It's a bloody overworked machine that's creaking at the seams and on the verge of blowing a gasket. That's what it is. You were meant to add another cylinder to our engine. From where I'm standing, you're turning out to be more of a dipstick. You're here to help solve problems, Elijah, not create them. Listen, I know how hard it is trying to fit into an established unit. Trust me on that one. But do you know what I found was the biggest thing that helped me integrate? Talk less, listen more. You've got one mouth and two ears. Don't come bulldozing your way in, expecting everyone to come round to your way of doing things. We all want you here. We need you here. But you have to slot in comfortably, not jam yourself in with a sledgehammer.'

Elijah nodded slowly. To Caroline, he certainly looked as if he'd been knocked down a few pegs.

'You're right. I'm sorry. If I'm honest, I think I'm probably just trying too hard.'

'It's often the way. I know it's not easy, Elijah. Especially when you're only here for a short while. But you're here to help us do a job. And while you're here, you're a part of the team as much as anyone else. The success of the team is as much your responsibility as everyone else's. We share the load, we work together and we treat each other with dignity and respect. That goes in all directions. For now, I think it's best if you just keep your head down for a while. Keep quiet in briefings, don't speak unless you're spoken to, and focus on following the information trails Detective Sergeant Antoine mentioned. Research, reveal, link. And let me know if you find anything.'

Elijah took a deep breath and gave one final nod. 'Got it.'

Caroline sighed and waved her hand towards him. 'Alright,' she said. 'Off you go.'

34

Dexter flopped onto his sofa and opened up his laptop as he leaned back, settling himself into the cushions.

He was feeling different today. A good sort of different. Something inside him knew he needed to capitalise on this sort of feeling, as it wouldn't be long before the other one was back.

Over the last few months and years, he'd researched all sorts of different options, but it was difficult when he didn't really know what was wrong. He'd considered going to see a therapist, but that had just caused more confusion than anything. Their websites and profiles all suggested they were the ideal people to help if you were feeling 'worried', 'anxious' or 'depressed', but none of these words quite seemed to fit, as far as Dexter was concerned. In any case, he wasn't sure he was a talker. He'd never been able to open up to anyone, and he didn't see why that would suddenly change now. Even if it did, why would a complete stranger, who was only there because they were getting paid, be the person to talk to?

He'd had friends who'd spoken openly about therapy and counselling and the good it had done them, so he could certainly see the appeal. But was it for him? He wasn't sure. He'd picked up a couple of self-help books, but found them trite and pretty rage-inducing. The idea that he could simply change his thoughts just by wanting to, or that chanting a few well-meaning affirmations into the mirror ten times each morning would fix him was frankly ludicrous. All Dexter knew was that the darkness inside him was deep. It wasn't something that could be medicated, talked or affirmed out of him. It would need far, far more than that. It was insidious.

He tried not to think too far along these lines as he typed another string of words into the search engine, hoping to find something new — something he hadn't come across before — an approach that would provide the key for him to unlock himself.

Covering it up had worked, up until a point. It didn't get rid of it, but it had at least kept it hidden. That'd had its drawbacks, of course. He'd had to keep well out of close relationships, for a start. He knew that if he ever let anyone get too close, there was no way he'd be able to hide that side of him from them. In any case, would it be right of him to want to? Surely the whole point of being with somebody was that you were meant to share those things and help each other?

Dexter had spent his life pondering these questions,

and was still no closer to an answer. Some days were better than others, but he was starting to realise he only had a finite amount of energy.

He'd tried all sorts. His first port of call, years earlier, had been to visit his GP. That had been a disaster, to say the least. The doctor had put him on antidepressants, which made him feel worse than he had before. Coupled with that, he'd started to gain weight at an obscene rate, which had done little to help his mood. They'd referred him for counselling and therapy, but by the time he'd reached the top of the waiting list ten months later he wasn't feeling too bad and was too busy with work to even think about taking them up on it. Throwing himself into his job worked well as a distraction, but that was about it.

He'd tried diet and lifestyle changes, choosing to eat more healthily and drink less alcohol, as well as joining a gym. He soon found he felt even more depressed at not being able to enjoy his favourite foods, and the gym membership became wasted as work and general life got in the way once again. Dexter estimated he must have spent hundreds, if not thousands of pounds on various self-help books and online courses designed to 'help you uncover the real you' and 'heal your past trauma', but found they'd done very little to help him.

He knew he needed professional assistance. Deep down, he accepted a therapist was probably the best option for him. Yes, he predicted they'd be useless and that he wouldn't open up to them, but what did he have to lose? He'd have spent a couple of hundred quid, wasted a few hours of his time and been proven right. But if his predictions were wrong and the sessions actually helped…? There was no telling what the potential benefits might be.

He loaded up the now-familiar website and typed his postcode into the *Location* box. The website asked him if he'd prefer sessions online or in person, and he selected the latter. If he was going to struggle to open up to someone under normal circumstances, he didn't see how it would be any easier to talk to a webcam. Having hit the *Search* button, a list of potential counsellors and therapists popped up — over three hundred of them within a fifteen mile radius of him. Down the left-hand-side of the website, a number of filters gave him options for narrowing down his search. He clicked the drop-down box under the heading *What's worrying you?* and was stunned at the number of options. Not knowing what to select, he instead used a few of the other filters to try and make his search a little easier.

Over the course of the next half an hour or so, Dexter looked at the profiles of more than a dozen counsellors and therapists. He wasn't entirely sure what he was looking for, or what most of the letters after their names meant. Some specialised in 'integrative therapy', whilst others talked about 'Human Givens' and 'acceptance and commitment therapy'. He jotted a few notes down on a notepad, then searched the web to find out what some of these terms meant. All he really wanted was to click a button, then have someone diagnose him and work out what type of therapy he needed. He hadn't expected to have to effectively triage himself.

A short while later, feeling he had a somewhat better idea as to the different types of therapy available, Dexter had narrowed his search down to three potential counsellors and therapists. If he was honest with himself, their photos had played a big part in his decision to get in touch with them. He knew it sounded weird, but he didn't think he'd be able to talk to anyone who didn't look 'nice'. He knew he was going to have to be vulnerable, and he wouldn't be able to do that if he didn't feel comfortable with the person he was talking to.

Ten minutes later, having sent an email to each of them, Dexter closed the lid of his laptop.

35

'She *what?*' Sara said, the pitch of her voice rising to a squeal as she digested what Elijah had just told her. 'She can't do that. That's outrageous!'

Elijah gave a small shrug and lifted the duvet up over his bare chest. 'Just the way it is. You can't blame her. You said she had a bee in her bonnet about EMSOU. It's probably just that. It'll pass.'

'She can't just put you on paperwork duties, though. That's a complete overreaction.'

Elijah shrugged again. 'It is what it is.'

'And she actually said she didn't want you to speak to any witnesses or access any existing records?'

Elijah lifted one shoulder slightly, then let it drop.

Sara shook her head in disbelief. 'That's ridiculous. She's the one who's been banging on about how short-staffed we are and how we needed another officer on the team. And the moment we get one, she goes and does this.'

'I can't really speculate. I shouldn't even be telling you this much,' Elijah replied.

'She told you not to talk about it? Jesus, it gets worse. You don't think she's going off the rails, do you? She's already taken a back seat on this case and left Dexter in charge. And I've seen how much pressure she's been under recently.'

Elijah took a deep breath and let out a sigh. 'I don't know, honey. It's not for me to say. I just thought you deserved to know the basics, that's all. As far as I'm concerned, I'm just going to keep my head down and get on with it. I don't want to cause a fuss.'

Sara put her hand on his arm. 'You're not causing a fuss at all. Some people just don't like change. I don't know why she's got such a problem with you. And Dexter, come to think of it. Then again, he's a man. He probably feels like his masculinity's threatened or something. Do you want me to have a word?'

Elijah's eyes narrowed. 'No. No, please. Like I said, I shouldn't have said anything to you in the first place. I don't want to cause any trouble. I just want everything to be peaceful and fine. After all the fun we've just had, I wouldn't want anything to ruin that. You were amazing.'

Sara smiled. 'So were you. You're amazing in so many ways. That's why I'm bloody furious at her for talking to you like that. She was the one who was so desperate to get someone new on the team.'

'Honestly, it's cool,' Elijah replied. 'She's probably just stressed out. You know how it is. I imagine she's got all sorts of pressure raining down on her from above, and perhaps things got on top of her a little. It's no big deal. Please don't cause a fuss, Sara.'

'I'm not going to. I wouldn't say anything, don't worry. I'm just making sure you're okay, that's all. You don't deserve to be treated like that.'

Elijah pulled Sara in a little closer and kissed her on the head. 'Thank you. Honestly, it means a lot that you're looking out for me. But I'll ride it out. Please don't say anything to anyone, though. It won't take them long to work out I told you, and then they'll be wondering why. It's probably not a good idea for everyone at work to know about us.'

'No, I agree,' Sara replied. 'It'll only put the gossip mill into overdrive.'

'Either that or Hills will use it as some sort of proof that I can't do my job properly. If she's in a bit of a funny mood at the moment, we don't want to be giving her anything that'll make life more difficult for everyone. Probably best we just keep it to ourselves for now. There'll be a time and a place. If we tell people a little way down the line, we'll be able to prove it hasn't and won't cause any issues at work by virtue of the fact no-one will have noticed.'

'True. I didn't think of it that way.'

Elijah's phone buzzed on the bedside table. He leaned

over and glanced briefly at the screen before kissing Sara on the head again.

'Anything important?' Sara asked.

'No, nothing. Just a spam email. Although, I have just seen the time, and I'm gonna have to get back for the dogs. If I leave it any longer they'll have wrecked my place.'

'Ah yeah, sorry. I can't wait to meet them.'

Elijah forced a smile. 'Yeah, it'll be good. Like I say, they're still pretty skittish at the moment, and don't take well to new people. Rescue dogs for you, I guess. As soon as they're a bit more sociable, I'll get you round. Got to do these things carefully. Wouldn't want one of them to bite that beautiful body of yours. That's my job.'

Sara squealed with delight. She couldn't remember the last time anyone had spoken to her like this.

'Will you pop over again tomorrow night?' she asked. 'I don't think I can get enough of you.'

'You try stopping me,' Elijah replied. 'Although maybe we can make it a little earlier? That way we can both get our fill before I have to dash off again.'

Sara smiled. 'Mmm. Sounds like a deal.'

36

In the cinema later that evening, Caroline felt her eyelids growing increasingly heavy as she tried to concentrate on the screen in front of her. The film was good, but it still wasn't enough to convince her brain it didn't need sleep.

She hadn't realised she'd nodded off until the ping of her mobile phone jolted her awake. Embarrassed, she grabbed it from her trouser pocket and flicked the switch to 'Silent' before whispering an apology to Mark.

She glanced down at the phone screen, shielding its bright light with her hand to ensure she didn't cause any further disturbances. It was Dexter.

Still not convinced about this Toni. Something doesn't quite fit. Think we need to probe further. Thoughts?

. . .

Before she could consider a response, her phone vibrated in her hand as another message landed, this time from Sara.

Apologies for the text, but didn't want to call as you mentioned you were out tonight. Found a link between Karlsen and the Norwegian power contract Clive T pulled out of. Karlsen's ex-wife worked for one of the financiers who was working on the deal. She's now married to a politician who works in the Ministry of Petroleum and Energy. Bit of a coincidence, no?

She tapped out a quick reply to Sara, then to Dexter. She kept both messages short and sweet, then returned her attention to the film.

Although now she was no longer on the verge of nodding off to sleep, before long she realised her attention had been pulled away from the screen and instead towards Dexter and Sara's messages. Had there been something odd about Toni? And Sara was right — that was one hell of a set of coincidences. But what did it all mean?

Before she could even think through the various permutations, her phone vibrated again in her pocket. She took it out and looked at the screen.

'Why don't you just go outside?' Mark asked, leaning over and whispering to her.

'Because I'm watching the film with you.'

'You're not, though, are you? You're on your phone.'

A woman in front of them turned her head slightly to the side — just enough for Caroline and Mark to see her disapproving look in profile, before she gave a slight and slow shake of the head and returned her gaze to the screen.

Caroline lowered her voice further. 'I can't help it if people message me, Mark.'

'I don't expect you to stop people messaging you. I expect you to be able to go an hour and a half without reading and replying to them.'

Caroline opened her mouth to reply, but stopped herself as the woman in front let out a deliberately audible sigh.

Mark looked at her and mouthed 'Just go.'

Caroline cocked her head sideways and looked at her husband; a silent communication that said everything she needed to say. Mark, though, refused to take his eyes from the screen.

Caroline stood up, making sure to clip the back of the woman's head with her bag as she did, and left the cinema.

37

Outside, Caroline tapped her phone and lifted it to her ear, waiting for Sara to answer.

'Hi. Film over already?' Sara asked.

'Yes and no,' Caroline replied. 'Long story. So, tell me everything we know.'

'Alright, but it's a bit complicated. So you remember Karlsen told us he was divorced? It turns out his ex-wife is linked with the Norwegian hydropower deal that Clive's company was involved with. It's a bit of a tenuous link to be honest, but at the time they were married, she worked for one of the firms that was helping to broker the deal. It's all hedge funds, corporate finance and stuff like that. Way over my head. They're quite a big company and seem to be involved in a lot of government contracts, so it might just be a coincidence, but it's got to be worth looking into.'

Caroline rubbed her head as she tried to take this all

in. 'And you said she's married to someone in government now?'

'A junior minister in the Ministry of Petroleum and Energy. Again, could be a coincidence. Like I say, her firm works on a lot of big government contracts. And it's Norway, so most of them involve oil and gas. It's quite likely they met through work.'

Caroline thought for a few moments. 'It's definitely interesting. But it still doesn't quite add up. What's the motive? If we're saying this is the background and the connection, and that Karlsen came over to kill Clive Thornton, it leaves one massive question. Why? Why would he want to help his ex-wife and her new partner? Why would either of them get Karlsen to do something like that, when presumably government ministers would have plenty of other ways of getting rid of someone? And what would getting rid of him achieve, anyway? The deal fell through years ago. Even if they blamed Clive Thornton, it makes no sense to have him killed.'

'Not enough sense, maybe. And you're right that it'd be really weird for Karlsen to be involved.'

Caroline nodded, even though Sara couldn't see it over the phone. 'I think my instinctive reaction was the same as yours. It seems like a big link at first, but is it really? Isn't it more likely that Karlsen, after his divorce, visits England for the umpteenth time and decides to head to one of the tourist hotspots he's not seen yet, and which just happens to be the workplace of a man who was tenuously linked to a business deal his ex-wife worked on years earlier?'

Sara was silent for a moment. 'When you put it like that, it does seem more likely.'

'Don't be disheartened, though,' Caroline said. 'It's great work, Sara. An impressive link to have uncovered, even if it doesn't go anywhere.'

'Oh, I can't take the credit for that,' Sara replied. 'It was Elijah who discovered the link. It came about through the admin work you put him onto. I bet he wasn't expecting to uncover something like that with it.'

Caroline took a deep breath and let it out slowly. 'No,' she said. 'No, I bet he wasn't.'

38

Sara gave a small yelp as she walked into the kitchenette area the next day and saw Aidan standing in the corner, leaning against the worktop.

'Christ, sorry,' she said, putting her hand to her chest. 'Didn't know you were in here. I must've been in a world of my own.'

Aidan shrugged. 'S'alright. Sorry if I scared you.'

'It's cool,' Sara replied, before making herself a cup of tea. 'You want one?'

'Nah, I'm good.'

Aidan was usually more friendly and talkative than this, so she could tell something was wrong. He only tended to get moody and brooding when he had something on his mind.

'Everything okay?' she asked, as casually as she could muster.

'Yeah, fine,' came the reply.

She turned to face him. 'You know I don't believe you, don't you?' she said.

Aidan looked back at her. She could see a look in his eyes — a feeling — one she could only describe as pain.

'You can talk to me,' she continued. 'If you need to, I mean. Or want to. I'm always happy to lend an ear. Anything you say won't be repeated to anyone else.'

Aidan gave a small smile out of the corner of his mouth. 'You really need to work on your arrest wording,' he said.

Sara smiled back. 'If I have to cuff you and book you in to get you to talk, I will.'

Aidan's smile faded as his mind moved back to the issue that was troubling him. He dropped his chin down towards his chest, took a deep breath, then looked back up at Sara.

'I've got a diary,' he said. 'Like a journal sort of diary, I mean. One I write in every day.'

'Aidan, I don't mean to prick your balloon, but I'm a DC. I've heard worse confessions than that.'

Aidan's smile briefly returned. 'Trust me,' he said. 'That's the easy bit.'

'Okay,' Sara said, picking up her mug, sensing he didn't want to volunteer any more information than this. 'Well, if you want to talk at any point, I'm here. I'm a good listener.'

Aidan's response came unexpectedly and suddenly.

'I found out Keira's been going through it. We broke up.'

Sara's jaw tensed slightly, although she wasn't sure why. 'Oh, Aidan,' she said. 'I'm sorry. What happened?'

Aidan took a deep breath and let out a loud sigh. 'The day before yesterday, just before I went to bed, I took it out of my bag and went to write in it, the same as I do every day. But when I opened it, I noticed that some of the loose scraps of paper at the back were in the wrong order. I mean, it's not as if there's a right order as such, but they weren't in the order I'd put them in. It was as if someone had opened it, not knowing the scraps were there, and had tried to put them back without knowing what order they'd been in originally.'

'And it definitely wasn't something you'd done yourself?'

'No. The scraps were notes I'd written when I didn't have the diary on me, or when I wanted to go back and add something at a later date. I've always been careful to keep them in the right order to make it easier for me to keep track. But this time some of them were upside down or the wrong way round. Someone else had put them back like that.'

'And you think it was Keira?'

'It must have been. She'd been over at mine that evening, but went home at nine because she said she was feeling ill. There was a good hour earlier that night where I'd been in the kitchen cooking dinner and she was in the living room watching telly. My bag was on the sofa, with the diary inside.'

'Do you keep it there all the time?'

'Yeah, I take it everywhere with me. I mean, I don't take it into the toilet or when I pop out to grab a pint of milk, but it comes to work with me, I take it on holiday, overnight stays, that sort of thing. It's therapeutic.'

'I see. Do you think that's why she left suddenly?'

Aidan shrugged. 'That's how it seems. She was fine before that. Said she felt a bit tired, but who doesn't when they get home from work?'

Sara thought for a few moments. 'I'm really not sure how to ask this, but is there anything in there that might have upset her if she'd read it?'

'Honestly? I don't know. I just sort of blurt my thoughts and feelings to get them out. I'm sure there've been days where I've been pissed off with her and will have written something to that effect, but everyone has days like that. Everyone has times where their partner annoys them.'

'True. But she might not have seen it like that at the time. It sounds like she just had an immediate instinctive reaction. Have you spoken to her since?'

'Yeah,' Aidan said, a sad look crossing his face. 'I had to. After I'd written in it that night, I used an old trick I remembered seeing in a book as a kid. I put a tiny dab of glue on each side of the opening, then stuck one of my hairs to it, so it wouldn't be immediately visible, but I'd know if anyone had opened the diary because the hair would be broken next time I went to write in it. Keira came over again the next night — yesterday — and seemed better. Like you said, I thought maybe she'd just seen something that'd taken her by surprise, and that she'd calmed down after sleeping on it. I decided not to say anything, but I'd already done the hair trick. Again, I left her in the living room with my bag after I came home from work, sorted dinner, had a shower. Then I came in, moved the bag and took the diary out.'

'And the hair was broken?'

'Yeah. She'd been going through it again. So I confronted her. At first she seemed shocked, which I put down to the surprise of being found out. But then she just got angry. Kept saying how could I accuse her of that, why would I do the trick with the hair if we were supposed to trust each other, that sort of thing. And I just thought, if she didn't do anything and she's trying to prove her innocence, why is she getting angry and throwing it all back at me, as if I'm the one in the wrong here? Anyway, when it came down to it I told her I couldn't trust her and she told me she couldn't be in a relationship where she wasn't trusted. So I guess that's that.'

'Oh Aidan. And there's definitely no-one else it could've been? Nowhere else you left the bag?'

'No, not at all. Like I say, I take it everywhere with me. It comes to work with me in the morning, then I bring it home. Both days, the bag was in the living room with Keira for at least an hour. I don't know, Sara. I just feel so... So crap.'

Sara reached out her arms to offer him a hug. 'Come here, you.'

Aidan stepped forward, and the pair embraced, Aidan letting out his pent-up tension as Sara calmly rubbed his back.

From a little further down the corridor, Elijah Drummond watched on.

39

Kelly paused as she felt her fingers grip the bedroom door handle. The brass warmed as she held it, working through her plan in her mind, just to make absolutely sure it wouldn't go wrong.

Her mum wouldn't be home for a while yet. Over the last few weeks, she'd come back at 2.57, 3.15, 2.51, 3.10 and 3.25. That averaged out to a little over seven minutes past three. If she wanted to be on the safer side, ten-to-three in the morning would about the earliest she could expect her.

She looked at the clock on her wall. Almost midnight. The numbers told her she had the best part of three hours, but she still couldn't shake the slightest hint of nervousness that had been creeping up inside her.

Doubt. That's what it was. The faint but increasingly present sense that the patterns and routines she'd got used to and found comfort in would be changed or blown apart at some point. It had been everything she hated. But at the same time, she had enough knowledge and acceptance that things could never go back to the way they were.

Her mind flashed back to the day the police arrived. Every time there was a knock at the door, Kelly would go over to her bedroom window, pull aside the net curtain and look down onto the driveway. Most of the time, it wasn't possible to see who was at the door, but on occasion she could. More often than not, she'd recognise cars on the driveway, or parked on the road outside. She knew her mum's, of course. And the neighbours'. FP71 DRF was the Amazon man. The last two weeks, Tesco's had delivered in AG21 HNN and KS70 PRP. But recently there'd been a new addition.

FR22 YCR never came onto the driveway. The Jaguar always stopped on the road, just short, its nose poking past the hedge as if it were hunting in the way of its animal namesake.

But not the first week.

The first time she saw FR22 YCR, it stopped right in front of the driveway. She couldn't see who was in it at first, but as the passenger door opened and her mum stepped out, the car's interior light seemed to bounce directly off his face, as if he'd been spotlit for a solo number in a stage show.

He hadn't looked up. Hadn't seen her. But the moment she'd seen him, she was transported back to that place, all those years ago. She remembered lying back on her bed, shaking and trembling as the memories came flooding back. She jumped and yelped a little as her mum came upstairs and opened Kelly's bedroom door. She didn't think her mum had noticed — nor was she able to see that Kelly's eyes were wide open and staring at the wall a mere six inches from her face — but she'd spotted the trembling and shaking immediately, even in almost complete darkness.

'A dream,' Kelly had said as her mother comforted her. 'I had a dream.'

It hadn't been wrong. It definitely wasn't a lie. It felt absolutely like a dream. A distant memory of a distant memory.

It had taken some time for Kelly to pluck up enough courage to tell her mum everything she remembered. She could still see the look in her eyes as she listened and took it all in. She didn't know what it meant, but it hadn't looked good.

She hadn't heard everything the police had said when they came over, but she'd picked up just about enough to get the gist. She'd seen enough TV shows to know the police came to speak to you when they thought you'd done something bad to a good person. The police helped good people and punished bad people. Her mother was a good person. He was a bad person.

That thought was enough for her to bring her hand down and open her bedroom door. With purpose, she walked down the stairs, took her shoes from the rack and put them on. She walked through to the kitchen and grabbed some spare change from the side. She didn't know if she'd need it, but she knew she had to be prepared. Walking back into the hallway, she reached up and grabbed the spare key from off the hook, inserted it into the lock and unlocked the door. Before she could stop to think, the door had closed behind her and she was on her way towards the centre of Oakham and the market square.

40

Later that evening, Dexter took a large mouthful of coffee as he waited for the video connection to load. When it did, the now-familiar face of Andreas Karlsen appeared on the screen.

'Mr Karlsen, good to see you again. Sorry it's so late.'

'That's okay,' Karlsen replied from his home in Norway. 'It's only late for you, remember. I'm quite used to my night shifts. I should be apologising to you for my work schedule keeping you up.'

'These things can't be helped. My colleague sitting next to me is Detective Constable Aidan Chilcott. He'll be taking notes based on the things we'll be covering. I understand you're alone and don't have anyone representing you or listening in?'

'That's correct,' Karlsen replied. 'I'm happy to talk freely and openly.'

'Alright. Again, sorry for the timing, but we wanted to

speak to you at the earliest possible opportunity because some new information has come to light and we think you might be able to help us. It's to do with your ex-wife, Eva. I understand you're divorced now, is that right?'

'Yes, that's correct.'

'What does Eva do for a living, Andreas?'

Karlsen let out a sigh. 'Honestly? Nowadays I'm not so sure. She keeps herself to herself. But she used to work in corporate finance, helping to broker big deals, mostly for the government and public sector bodies. I'm guessing you're asking me this because she was linked to the hydroelectric project that Clive Thornton's company was involved with?'

'That's right,' Dexter replied. 'Can you tell me more about that, please?'

'Well, she was involved with organising the funding and finance. That's what she did for a living. I never fully understood it, but these sorts of infrastructure projects obviously can't happen without significant levels of finance.'

'And your involvement was what, exactly?'

'I had no involvement.'

'Are we expected to believe that?'

'You can believe what you wish. I can only tell you the truth.'

Dexter paused for a moment. 'Has Eva remarried, Andreas?'

'She has.'

'Who to?'

'I think you already know who to. Tomas Askvik.'

'And what does he do for a living?'

'He's a politician. He's a junior in the Ministry of Petroleum and Energy. But as I say, I think you already know that.'

'We do have to check things and ensure everyone's on the same page,' Dexter replied. 'So let me get this straight. Your ex-wife, who was one of the people in charge of arranging the corporate finance for this enormous government project in Norway, is now married to a junior minister in the Ministry of Petroleum and Energy — the department responsible for those sorts of projects. And on the day the man who was effectively responsible for collapsing the deal dies, you just happened to be in the same small town in the middle of England, in the very building he works in. Have I got that right?'

'I don't see any inaccuracies in any of that information,' Karlsen replied.

'You came over to see him, didn't you?'

Karlsen took a long breath in, then let it out before speaking.

'No. That is the truth. My reasons for coming over to England were honest and noble, as I already told you. Did I know about Clive Thornton? Yes. Did I know he lived in that approximate area? Yes. Did I expect to bump into him? No.'

'And when you did, did you intentionally return on the day he died in order to speak to him?'

Karlsen was silent for a few moments. 'It isn't quite

that simple,' he said, eventually. 'I don't know what I thought, if I'm honest. When the hydroelectric deal collapsed, Eva was distraught. She'd worked night and day to get it to the point she had. We'd been going through our own stresses and issues, too, but that was what tipped things over the edge. Listen, I couldn't give a damn about the energy deal. But in my own way I suppose I blamed Clive Thornton for being the final ingredient in ending my marriage. Of course, he'll never have known that. He had no involvement in my marriage, at least not directly. But there's no doubt in my mind that the stress and anxiety he caused was what finally flipped that switch. But that was all in the past, you understand. I had no reason to want to kill him. I'm a much happier person now I'm divorced. I'm finally free to be me. Of course, I didn't see it that way at the time, but I guess that's irrelevant. My motive for seeing him was purely curiosity. He never knew who I was. He didn't need to. But maybe it was just one of those things I felt I needed to lay to rest. In any case, I am not responsible for his death, I can assure you of that. I completely understand how it looks, and I can see why you might think that, but it just isn't the case.'

Dexter was still digesting this information when there was a knock at the door. Sara, who was also working late, entered. Dexter muted the video call.

'What's up, Sara?' he asked.

'Sarge, we've just had a call come in. I think you're going to want to hear this.'

'Alright. We'll just be a little while longer here, is that okay?'

Sara glanced at the computer screen, then back at Dexter. 'Honestly? If I were you, I wouldn't waste your time talking to Karlsen. I think we've got our killer.'

41

Caroline squinted as she shielded her eyes from the bright kitchen lights. For the first time, she found herself silently agreeing with Mark that they should have installed dimmables.

'Okay, Dex,' she mumbled into her phone as she pulled her dressing gown tighter around her with her free hand. 'Start again.'

Dexter's voice sounded far more animated than hers, and the fact he'd called her at this hour told her everything she needed to know about the seriousness of the situation.

'We received a call from Toni Scott's daughter, Kelly. She phoned it in on the nines, and it was passed through to 101, then on to us. The call came from a phone box in the market square in Oakham. In short, Kelly has made an allegation of historic abuse towards her by Clive Thornton.'

At first, Caroline didn't realise she'd been holding her breath. She let out a long exhalation, then blinked as she tried to get her brain to switch back to a functioning level.

'What sort of abuse?' she asked, her voice still hoarse.

'Sexual. We're going to have to get a full statement from her and tape an interview to get the details, but it throws a whole new load of light on things. Toni told us she'd only met Clive far more recently, but if he'd been involved in abusing her daughter in childhood, how can that be true? And more to the point, does it give Toni a motive for murder?'

'I'd say it definitely does, yeah. But we'd have to prove she knew about it.'

At the other end of the phone, Dexter let out a disappointed sigh. 'Don't tell me you think this is just another coincidence.'

'I don't think anything, Dex. I'm just saying, it'd be up to us to prove Toni knew about the allegations of abuse. What was said on the 101 call? Do you have a transcript?'

'Just that something had happened in the past, and that Clive had done something to her that she knew was bad. The operator did try to probe a little, and managed to ascertain that it was sexual and needed police attention, but didn't get any details. Weird thing is, Kelly explicitly asked if she could speak with me. Apparently I seemed "nice" when I was at the house.'

'Well, perhaps you should start being more of a git. Sounds like you're just giving yourself more work.'

'We're going to need to tread carefully as it is. Kelly's… difficulties… mean we're going to need to do things slightly differently. We can't have her mum there, for obvious reasons. But she's going to need someone. Usually, I'd recommend we sit in the next room and watch the feed, but if she's said she wants me there… I dunno. If she trusts me. If it means she's more likely to talk.'

'I see what you're saying, Dex. One-on-one always works best, and the more people there, the less likely she'll be to talk freely. But you can't be the one-on-one. At the very least, it needs a specialist officer and probably another adult because of her needs.' Caroline scratched her head. 'Oh Jesus. We've got the logistics of even *getting* to Kelly to sort out first.'

'I was thinking that myself,' Dexter replied. 'We can't go round while Toni's there, as it'll spook her. The whole situation with Kelly's special needs is too delicate. Toni could pull the "responsible adult" card and cause us all sorts of issues. It'll need to be while she's out.'

Caroline looked at the date on her watch. 'Today would be perfect,' she said. 'Toni's routine is like clockwork. She'll be at work today, and going to the supermarket on her way home. That should give us plenty of time to bring Kelly in, get a full statement and have enough behind us to bring Toni in for questioning.'

'It's a big gamble,' Dexter said, cocking his head. 'What if she clams up, says nothing and blurts out to her mum that she's been to see the police?'

'And what if she doesn't, Dex? What if we don't bring her in? We have an obligation to the truth. In any case, if we haven't got what we need out of Kelly by the time Toni's back home, we can pick her up too. That'll give us another twenty-four hours with the two separated.'

Dexter clenched his jaw and shook his head slightly. 'I dunno. What if Toni comes home early?'

'We'll make sure we've got someone stationed nearby. They can pick her up and bring her in before she's even had a chance to think about it. Look at the facts, Dex. We've got a serious historic allegation of sexual abuse against a minor with special needs. Kelly realises her mum — who dotes on her — is now seeing this man, tells her about it, and the next thing you know the guy's been murdered.'

'What happened to following the evidence and forming conclusions from that?' Dexter asked.

'That's exactly what I'm doing. This allegation is a huge piece of evidence. We all know what's happened here, Dex. The background might be considered circumstantial. The fact Toni's DNA was on Clive's body and clothes can easily be explained away by their affair. But if we can get evidence that places her at the scene, or even ruffle her feathers enough to get a confession, we're laughing. I fancy my chances on the confession, personally. Look at the circumstances. Her daughter's been abused. She's not a violent woman, but that was enough to drive her to bludgeon a man to death. That's not the sort of emotion you can hide easily. If we can stir that up again, there's no way she'll be able to hold it back. We're not looking at a criminal mastermind here, Dex. But it's your job. It's your shout.'

Dexter sighed quietly. 'Alright,' he said. 'Okay. Let's get everyone in place. Let's do it.'

42

Dexter stepped out of his car and onto Toni Scott's driveway. He couldn't deny there was a certain buzz about the clandestine way in which they were doing this, but it also made him nervous as hell. There was a lot at stake — a lot on the line — and he couldn't afford to mess this up.

He rang the doorbell, then took a few steps back, knowing that Kelly would peer out of her bedroom window the moment she heard the bell.

He didn't look up — he didn't want to spook her or alarm her. She had to do this on her own terms, in her own time.

A few moments later, he heard the muted thud of footsteps on the stairs inside the house. A couple of seconds later, the door opened.

'Hi, Kelly,' Dexter said, showing her a beaming smile. 'Do you remember me?'

'Yes, you're the policeman,' Kelly replied.

'I am indeed. How would you like to come and have a tour of a real-life police station?'

Kelly's face briefly flashed excitement, then settled itself. 'I'd need to ask my mum. I'm not allowed to go out without her. I need to wait for her to get home.'

'Don't worry about that,' Dexter said, smiling again. 'I promise you we've got it all sorted out already.' He held out his hand. 'Are you excited?'

Kelly looked at his hand, then back up at him. 'Yeah,' she said as a smile broke out across her face. 'Let's go!'

43

The first thing Caroline noticed as she watched the screen in front of her was how calm Kelly Scott seemed to be. There was definitely an underlying edge of nervousness — a fear of the unknown — but Caroline would have expected someone with her condition to be in full-blown panic mode. Interestingly, it was something she'd seen a few times before when watching interviews with victims of sexual abuse. Sometimes dragging up the painful memories in such a clinical and formal environment would cause rising panic and complete meltdowns. On other occasions, it seemed to provide just enough emotional distance for them to tell their story in a calm and matter-of-fact way.

The psychology of these types of cases had always fascinated her. Worryingly, although the victims of sexual assault who were calmer in their interviews tended to be able to provide more critical and damning evidence that could be used in court, the sight of a victim talking calmly about being sexually abused did something unfortunate to a jury — and often even a judge. It was as if victims weren't fully believed — or believed at all — unless they were in a wailing heap on the floor.

In Caroline's experience, there was no correlation whatsoever between the victim's emotional response and whether or not the incident had happened. False allegations were thankfully rare, and where she'd encountered them she'd found no correlation with how dramatic or emotional the person's response had been. The truth was, everyone reacted in different ways. Their unique psychological makeup would dictate their response — nothing else. She'd come to realise and accept that every person had a different response to trauma, in the same way they did to everything else. One person seeing an empty crisp packet on a pavement might end up in a foul mood for the rest of the day, condemning the youth of today to hell and damnation, cursing the state of the country. Another might not even notice it. Was either perspective right or wrong? No. Which one was factual? Neither. Both. The only incontrovertible fact was that there was a crisp packet on the floor. Everything else that happened was a reaction — a process inside the mind. A choice.

Psychology had fascinated her for as long as she could remember. She'd often wondered if it had been one of the reasons she'd been so keen to get involved in the police. Everyone processed the information in front of them in vastly different ways, and she'd seen that in every facet of the job. From breaking the news to parents that their child had been murdered, to arresting a violent criminal who'd been free from apprehension for decades. Whatever the situation, some people would react dramatically, their fight-or-flight response causing them to either enter a state of absolute denial or to have a complete emotional meltdown. Conversely, others would simply sit down and put out their hands to be cuffed, or nod silently as they realised they'd never see their loved one again. No response was right or wrong; it was simply theirs. The key was in recognising which aspects were factual information and which were mere emotional responses shaped by the life they'd lived.

Caroline had lost count of the number of articles she'd read in newspapers, or items she'd heard on radio phone-ins, where allegations of historic sex abuse were discounted purely because they were historic. It was as if some sections of society had decided that a victim of the most horrifying assault only deserved to be heard if they asserted their right within an arbitrarily determined period of time, as if justice were a Tesco voucher. There seemed to be no recognition of the fact that some events were so horrific and traumatic to the victims that their brains simply didn't know how to cope with it, and reacted by pushing it right to the back in a frantic effort to survive. And who was to decide what was traumatic 'enough' for any given victim? Only them. Only they had lived life as they had. Only they saw the world through their lens.

The very nature of sexual abuse, the people who committed it and the victims they chose, all had the unfortunate but common result that those who were impacted worst felt they couldn't speak out. It was the natural conclusion of what was essentially a grossly warped power dynamic. How many young women, at an age where they're only just discovering the world and its many ways, would feel able to speak out against a powerful celebrity or person in a position of authority? It was no coincidence that the bus driver, cleaner or creepy old man down the street was more likely to be reported and convicted of sexual abuse than a celebrity, police officer or headteacher. And it certainly wasn't because those in the latter three professions had a lower propensity to abuse.

Regardless, Caroline knew the burden of proof for historic sex offences was much higher than for recent events, but it was also — for obvious reasons — far more difficult to obtain that proof. Footprints, DNA and CCTV footage would be long gone. Memories would have faded just the same. Witnesses, confidants and sometimes even perpetrators would have long since left this earth. And before any of these hurdles had even been considered, those who'd been tasked to judge and deliver justice would already be primed to doubt the veracity of the case before they'd even heard it.

For Caroline, this was a classic example. A girl with learning difficulties, a successful businessman who'd dedicated his life to charitable causes and who'd since died, and allegations that stretched back decades. In this particular case, though, Caroline was less worried. She had a feeling that legal justice for the abuse was less important — not to mention futile now that Clive Thornton was dead. If the puzzle pieces were falling together in the way she thought they were, justice had already been done. Her task now was to confirm that, prove it beyond all reasonable doubt and close that chapter of the book for once and for all.

Caroline wondered how much Dexter's presence in the room had calmed Kelly. She'd asked for him specifically, and although she didn't seem too concerned that Alyson Marlor, the specialist safeguarding officer, was leading the conversation and asking all the questions, Caroline had noticed that Kelly seemed to turn to Dexter before answering, as if for reassurance. In that moment, but certainly not for the first time, she felt thankful to have him on her team. He was a calming and reassuring presence for everyone, and so often injected humour and warmth into what might otherwise be a more stressful and exhausting environment.

'Do you find it difficult to remember what happened, Kelly?' Alyson asked.

Kelly glanced briefly at Dexter before answering. 'Not anymore,' she said.

'How do you mean?'

'I didn't really remember at all. Not for a long time. But then I did.'

'And what made you remember?'

'When I saw him. When he dropped Mum home. I

hadn't seen him since I was twelve, but I knew it was him straight away. I recognised him. And he has the same name. He was in his car. FR22 YCR.'

'We have been able to confirm that the Clive Thornton your mum knew was the same Clive Thornton who volunteered at the Girl Guides group you used to attend,' Dexter said, interrupting proceedings momentarily.

'I know,' Kelly replied. 'I know it was him.'

'Are you okay if we talk about those times?' Alyson asked. 'About when you attended Girl Guides.'

Kelly nodded.

'Okay. Tell me what you remember. Do you recall which evenings you used to go? Who took you? Who else was there? Where it was?'

Kelly swallowed and then spoke. 'It was on Thursdays. At the church hall. Mum took me. There wasn't anybody else to take me. There were other girls there. Holly Walmsley. Nicole Coulson. Steph McEwan. Kelly Dowling. I remember her because she had the same first name as me.'

'And do you still keep in touch with any of these girls?'

Kelly shook her head. 'No. I don't really have friends. Only my mum.'

Caroline felt her breath catch in her chest as she watched on.

'And what was Clive Thornton's role at the Guides group? What sort of jobs did he do?' Alyson asked.

'Helped out. All sorts, really. Setting up activities.

Taking groups off to do things. He organised the camping trips.'

'Can you tell me a little more about the camping trips?'

'We used to go to the woods. I didn't like it. Tents scare me. I didn't want to go in it. So he said I could stay with him in his hut.'

'Okay. So he was staying in a hut? Was it nearby?'

'Yes. It was near the tents.'

'And where were the other adults sleeping?'

'In tents.'

'And Clive Thornton was the only one who was staying in the hut?'

'Yes. And me.'

'Okay. So he said you could stay with him in his hut, and you did, yes? What happened next, Kelly?'

Caroline watched and listened as Kelly spoke, recalling every last detail with horrifying accuracy. And somewhere deep inside Caroline, another little light went out.

44

Sara breathed in deeply, feeling the chill winter air biting at the edges of her nostrils as she crossed her arms more tightly in an attempt to keep out most of the cold.

She'd never been a smoker herself, but she'd found an odd attachment to those moments where her smoker friends would step outside for a couple of quiet minutes, whatever the weather. It was something she still tended to do even when on her own — minus the cigarettes, of course. Whereas her friends who smoked had associated the chance to take two minutes to decompress with the quick hit of nicotine, Sara had associated it with stepping outside for a short period of time.

She wasn't alone for long, though, as the door opened and Elijah stepped out, walking towards her. He seemed to have a slight hunch to his shoulders, and was moving with less confidence and assurance than he usually did.

'You okay?' she asked.

'I'm not sure really,' he replied, avoiding eye contact with her.

Sara stepped towards him, keen to show she cared, but also not to break their rule of being too "obvious" at work. 'Can I help?'

'I don't know. Maybe. Probably.'

By now, the body language was clear to Sara. 'Elijah, have I done something to upset you?' she asked.

Elijah let out a small sigh. 'I saw you in the kitchen with Aidan. I saw you... hugging.'

Sara thought back. 'Oh. Yeah. He was upset about something, so I gave him a hug. It didn't mean anything.'

Elijah looked up at her for the first time. Sara could see pain in his eyes. 'It looked like more than that,' he said.

'It really wasn't. He was just upset, that's all.'

Elijah swallowed. 'I'm sorry,' he said. 'It just... I've been hurt before, you know? I can't bear the thought of that happening again. Not with you.'

Sara put a hand on his upper arm and rubbed gently. 'Hey, I know. You don't need to worry. I'm not going to hurt you. I can understand how it might have looked, especially if you've been hurt in the past, but I'm looking you in the eyes and promising you I'd never do anything like that, Elijah.'

He was silent for a few moments, then began to talk. 'I know. I'm sorry. I shouldn't have even mentioned it or thought anything of it. It's just really hard when you've been burnt in the past. My brain plays these tricks on me.

I guess it's just trying to protect me and make sure I'm not hurt again.'

'You won't be,' Sara replied. 'Not by me, anyway. You honestly have nothing to worry about.'

'But those things you said at the pub. About him. Not knowing if you were over him.'

'I said I sometimes wondered. But I don't anymore.'

'Are you sure?' he asked, tears forming at the corners of his eyes.

Sara stepped towards him and rested her forearms on his shoulders, locking her hands behind his neck.

'I'm sure.'

A few moments later, their kiss came to an end as they each remembered their pledge to remain professional at work.

'Are you okay?' Sara asked.

Elijah nodded. 'Yeah.'

'And are we okay?'

Elijah nodded again, and smiled. 'Yeah,' he said. 'Yeah, we're just fine.'

45

Although they'd deliberately chosen to speak to Kelly at a time they knew her mum would be out of the house, Caroline and Dexter had judged that they couldn't be too careful. As a result, they had stationed Aidan to keep an eye on Toni, reporting her movements and getting ready to alert them should she look as if she were heading home. If it looked like they were going to be caught short, the backup plan was for Aidan to approach Toni and bring her in for further questioning. In any case, they were pretty certain there would be further questions they'd need to ask her.

They were already familiar with Toni's routine, and they knew she was due to leave work at six o'clock that evening, before heading to the Aldi supermarket just off the Oakham bypass. All in all, it was shaping up to be a pretty boring afternoon for Aidan.

He sat in his car, keeping Toni's vehicle in his eye-line

as he played game after game of Candy Crush on his phone, trying desperately to pass the time. Although he didn't consider himself to be the most active and dynamic person in the world, sitting in the car listening to an endless loop of rubbish radio and scrolling through his phone was not exactly his idea of fun.

The worst thing was that this was precisely the sort of situation in which he instinctively wanted to call Keira. The pair could easily spend a couple of hours nattering away on the phone about nothing much, sharing stories about their days or just getting to know each other better. There hadn't been a moment where they'd been bored or the conversation would grow stale. But that wouldn't be possible anymore.

He'd felt awful about confronting Keira, but he knew he'd had no choice. For him, trust was the most fundamental aspect of any relationship, and if Keira had done something to break that trust — or if he had good reason to suspect as much — he felt it was only right that he should bring it up.

To say it hadn't gone down well would be an understatement. If Aidan thought he'd felt violated and upset at the thought of Keira reading his diary, it was nothing compared to how Keira seemed to feel about being accused of it. Her response had been a little dismissive at first, as if she hadn't really understood what he was asking, and certainly hadn't grasped the seriousness of the situation from Aidan's perspective. But when he'd pressed her on the matter, she seemed to simultaneously explode and implode.

Her reaction had swayed between anger and devastation, with moments of blaming him for being some sort of ogre to believe such a thing, and complete internal torment at being on the receiving end of the accusation. She hadn't known which way to turn, it seemed, and neither had he. But one thing had been made clear: the relationship was over.

That realisation was what had hit Aidan hardest. He found relationships hard as it was, but he couldn't deny he'd got extraordinarily attached to Keira. Whichever way he looked at it, she was the most incredible woman he'd ever met. She'd changed his way of thinking about things, and made him look at life in a completely different way. He couldn't even put his finger on most of it, but it was as if she was an angel sent from above to change his life. And now, although his life had been changed in any case, the cruellest thing was that he wouldn't get to share that with her.

He hadn't been in the best place recently. Keira hadn't seen the best of him by any stretch of the imagination. Since he'd suffered heartbreak in his previous relationship when his partner had decided to move to Australia, his head hadn't been in the right place. He hadn't intended to meet Keira so quickly, and certainly hadn't meant to fall in love. But he had. The fallout in his head had been immense, and Keira had unfortunately borne the brunt of that. Not only had she been in the right place at the wrong time, but she'd been the only person Aidan had ever felt he could open up to.

What felt so cruel now was that he had just got himself to a place where he felt secure and comfortable in himself, and could feel his inner engines revving, ready to power down the track and leave his past in his wake. And it was just at that moment that everything had collapsed.

He'd put everything into his relationship with Keira. Emotionally speaking, he was entirely invested. He'd given it everything he had at the time. And now he had a whole lot more to give. She'd been an absolute angel to him, more patient than he'd ever had any right to expect, and it hurt so much to realise that they'd fallen short at the very last hurdle. There was no way he could make Keira see that, of course. As far as she was aware there could have been a hundred thousand more hurdles after that one. It didn't matter that he knew there wasn't — that he was the only one who could possibly know. There was always going to be a point at which she'd pull the plug, but the biggest sting was the timing. Just another week, a few more days, and she would've seen the change in him.

He felt himself welling up, as he so often did now. He'd cried almost every hour since, trying desperately to hold himself together and distract himself with work, but it was no good. Fortunately, he'd managed to keep it hidden from most people. He didn't want them seeing how absolutely crushed he was by what had happened. And he certainly didn't want anyone knowing what an idiot he'd been.

He knew what people would say. *It'll get easier. Time is a great healer. You just need some space. You'll look back on this very differently in a year's time.* He didn't care. He wasn't a year down the line. He was in the here and now, and here and now it hurt like hell. Life without Keira just didn't seem possible. She'd made such an impact on his life, had become so central to his very being, it seemed inconceivable now to have a life without her. But no matter how he felt, he knew it wouldn't make a difference. Once Keira made her mind up about something, that was that. It was to her own detriment, he knew. She would certainly cut off her nose to spite her face. But the truth was they'd both changed each other in their own ways during the time they'd been together, and Aidan hoped — prayed — that he'd softened her just enough that she might alter a lifelong habit and consider that perhaps she could have made the wrong decision.

The trouble was, he knew she had to miss him. As much as he wanted to stay in contact and talk to her, it wouldn't do any good. If he kept being the one going to her, there would never be anything to make her take that step forward. All she'd have to do is sit back and either fend off his approaches or accept them. And while he was the one doing the doing, it was inevitable those approaches would be fended off. The only possible solution was to give her space — space to think, and also the space that he would leave in her life. Only once that gap was visible and obvious would she begin to miss what had previously been there. And only then could any potential rebuilding begin.

Although he knew that made sense logically, Aidan

couldn't deny how much it hurt to come to that realisation. Not being able to text her to say good morning, to ask how her day had been, to send her daft and silly images he'd found on Facebook — it all left a massive hole in his life, and a gaping chasm in his soul. He didn't know how long that would take to heal. It felt as if it never would.

The scariest thought of all, though, was that she might not miss him. She might well notice the gap where he'd been and realise that she actually quite liked it, as if she'd got rid of a piece of old furniture that was only cluttering up the room anyway. And there was always the possibility that she'd spot a better piece of furniture somewhere else and decide to put that in her room instead. These were all huge, enormous risks. Keira was an incredibly attractive woman, and she'd certainly have absolutely no trouble finding someone else in a heartbeat. She could have her pick of any man she wanted to. That meant all Aidan could do was hope she didn't want to.

He reached across and changed the radio station, hoping to jolt himself out of what was otherwise in danger of becoming a depressive episode. Whichever station he switched to, he seemed to find the same bland mix of music that appeared to be everywhere. Eventually, he switched the radio off and let out a deep sigh. He knew it was no good getting lost in his thoughts. But that didn't make it any easier, and it certainly didn't mean he could just switch them off at will.

Fortunately for him, he was soon jolted out of his mental torture. Seeing movement out of the corner of his eye, his attention was diverted to the sight of Toni Scott leaving her work premises and strolling towards her car. Without missing a beat, he picked up the phone and called Dexter.

'Sarge, we've got movement. She's just getting into her car as we speak.'

'Alright,' Dexter replied. 'Can you see which way she's heading?'

'Not yet. One moment.' Aidan watched as Toni's car reversed out of its space then headed towards the car park's exit. There was a brief moment before the indicator light flashed on and the car positioned itself to turn left. 'She's heading left,' he said into the phone. 'Confirm — she's turning left.'

'Not towards home?' Dexter asked.

'No. It looks as if she's heading to the supermarket.'

'Thanks, Aidan,' Dexter replied. 'Will hand over to the others.'

Aidan ended the call and put his phone back in his pocket. Then he closed his eyes and relaxed back into his car seat.

46

Hearing victims' accounts never got any less harrowing for Dexter, and he took a deep breath as he left the room and sat down with her in another, similar — but, crucially, different — one.

'How are you feeling, Kelly?' he asked.

'I'm okay.'

'You did very well in there. You've got a real memory for details. You should be a police officer.'

'I've always thought about that, but Mum says I'm not right for the world of work.'

Dexter gave a smile. 'It sounds like your mum really looks after you.'

Kelly nodded. 'She always has. She's all I've got. And she says I'm all she's got.'

'I can understand that,' Dexter replied, sadness tinging his voice. 'But you don't need to worry. We'll look after you. All of this is to help you and your mum. You know that, don't you?'

Kelly nodded again.

Dexter watched as her nod began to slow.

'Do you promise?' she asked.

'Absolutely.'

'Because I don't ever want to stop playing Run Home.'

'Run Home?'

'It's a board game. You have four coloured men and you have to go round the board and get them all back in their home spaces before the other person does, but you can't do it until you roll a six.'

Dexter smiled and nodded. 'I think I know the one. We used to call it Ludo in our house.'

Kelly shrugged.

'Do you like playing Run Home, then?'

'Yes, I love it. I always play it with Mum. It's our favourite thing to do together. So far I'm winning by one hundred and sixty two games to one hundred and forty, but Mum's catching up so I need to make sure I get better at it.'

Forcing another smile, Dexter changed the subject slightly. 'Are there any other games you like to play? We've got a few here somewhere, I think.'

'No.'

'Alright. No worries.'

'Mum likes gardening, but I don't.'

'Oh?'

'It makes me dirty. I tried it once, but I don't like it.'

'That's fair enough. Does she grow lots of plants and flowers?'

'Yes. Once she even did it at night time.'

Dexter's ears pricked up slightly. 'Really?' he asked.

'Yes, it was very recently. She came home late one night and went straight round the side gate and into the garden. I thought she might have forgotten her key, but she went into the shed and got a spade out, and she dug a hole in the flower bed and planted something in it. Nothing's grown yet, so I don't know what it will be, but sometimes it can take a while for the plants to grow, especially when it's winter. That's why you shouldn't plant things in winter.'

Dexter nodded slowly as the pieces started to come together in his mind.

'Yeah,' he said. 'Yeah, I think I'd tend to agree.'

47

'I knew policing in Rutland would be a bit different to regional major crime, but I didn't realise it was this exhilarating,' Elijah quipped. 'I mean, how do you guys handle the adrenaline rush that comes with sitting in a supermarket car park of an evening?'

'If we get too excited, we just take a shot of heroin,' Sara quipped in return. 'But to be honest, it's not usually this exciting. Sometimes we watch people put their bins out instead.'

'Christ. I don't know how you manage to wind down at night. That'd be too much drama for me.'

The pair hadn't been sitting in the Aldi car park for long, but in many ways it had felt like an age. For Sara, though, any time spent with Elijah seemed to fly by. She'd never felt as comfortable in someone else's company as she did with him, and she smiled inwardly to herself as she enjoyed the lighthearted back-and-forth between them.

She glanced over at Toni Scott's car, one row over and about six cars down from them. It was just far enough away that they could keep an eye on her and her movements without being spotted, but they were also perfectly positioned to block off the entrance to the car park should they need to.

'So, tell me an interesting fact about yourself. Something completely random,' Elijah said, breaking the brief silence.

'Completely random? You've put me on the spot now,' she replied. 'Uh, I've only ever lived in two houses. Does that count?'

'Not really.'

Sara laughed. 'Alright, alright. I once had three different animals defecate on me in one day. Does that count?'

Elijah raised an eyebrow. 'It certainly warrants elaboration,' he said.

'I went out for lunch with a friend. This was a couple of years ago. She'd just had a new baby. Anyway, we're in Caffè Nero in town, and I'm sitting there cuddling her little one when it lets rip with what I thought was the most almighty fart of all time. We're sitting and chatting, and about a minute or so later I just see my friend's eyes slowly moving towards my arm, and then her jaw drops. So I look down, and the arm of my white jumper is now brown.'

'Amazing.'

'So there's no way I can wear this jumper anymore,

and all I've got on underneath is a little strappy top. And it's February. So I take the jumper off and I shove it in an empty carrier bag, apologise to my friend and I head off home. Anyway, I'm about a hundred yards down the road when a bird craps on my back. In my hair, the whole lot. By this point I swear I'm cursed. So I get home, I shower three times, I put my clothes on a four-hour boil wash, and I climb into bed, thinking at least I'm safe there. Little while later, my cat comes in and curls up on my stomach. I'd say that lasted maybe thirty seconds, then he just stands up, squats slightly, curls one out on my chest and walks off as if nothing happened.'

Elijah had been trying to hold his laughter back, but it was no use.

'Oh wow,' he said. 'Yeah, okay. I wasn't expecting that answer. I like how that's the interesting fact about yourself that you think of first, though.'

'To be fair, the first one I thought of was that I've only ever lived in two houses. So I'm not *completely* weird.'

'Still, that's a story that's got to come out in the wedding speech,' Elijah replied, chuckling and then immediately stopping in his tracks. 'Sorry. I didn't mean...'

'It's fine,' Sara replied, looking out of the window at the side of the car.

'I just meant...'

'It's okay. I know what you meant. It was just a throwaway comment. Don't worry.'

Elijah reached across and took hold of her hand.

'I really do like you, Sara,' he said.

Sara looked back at him.

'I like you too.'

Before another word could be said, Elijah leaned across and began to kiss her.

48

Back in Caroline's car, Dexter had barely said a word since leaving Toni Scott's house.

'Everything okay?' Caroline asked, as casually as she could muster, finding his uncharacteristic silence a little unnerving.

'I dunno,' Dexter replied, his mind clearly elsewhere. 'I just feel awful lying to Kelly, that's all. Especially after everything she's been through, and how she specifically wanted me there.'

'You didn't lie. You told her we'd look after her mum.'

'Yeah, but I think her idea of "looking after" someone is very different to ours. I don't think a prison breakfast was quite the idea of hospitality she had in mind.'

'We don't know for sure she's done anything yet. It could all just be another big coincidence for all we know.'

Dexter started to shake his head. 'Nah. I think we both

know what's happened. Toni got involved with Clive, who Kelly then recognised as the man who'd abused her when she was younger. She tells her mum, who reacts by killing him.'

'But why?' Caroline asked. 'Why not just report it to the police and let us deal with it? Committing pre-meditated murder is a pretty drastic response for someone with no history of a violent past whatsoever.'

Dexter shrugged. 'Because she knew nothing would come of it. We all know how difficult it is to prove historic sex offences. You throw a girl with special needs into that mix as the victim, plus the likelihood of a defence barrister angling that the daughter's just jealous Mum has another man, and the chances of getting any sort of result are close to nothing. What jury's going to convict on that? It wouldn't even get past the CPS.'

'Toni Scott's DNA was found at the scene.'

'Yeah, on and around Clive. Which is where she'd spent most of the past few months anyway, by the sounds of things. It certainly doesn't place her at the scene beyond reasonable doubt.'

'Well, we'll have a better idea once we've spoken to her. But listen Dex, please don't worry about Kelly. You absolutely did the right thing. Everyone will be better off for it. If Toni is guilty, justice will prevail. The universe has a wonderful way of making things right.'

'You're not the first person I've heard say that,' Dexter replied. 'But there's no way to prove that, is there?'

'How do you mean?'

'The universe always making things right, I mean. It makes things as they are. What happens happens. As humans, all we do is adjust to what's happened and make that our new normal. And after a while it feels normal, too. It doesn't mean it was the "right" chain of events, or that an alternative outcome wouldn't have been better for everyone involved.'

Caroline let out a deep breath. 'I think we're getting a little too philosophical for work, aren't we?'

Dexter shrugged. 'Our work *is* life. It's people's lives. Their fates. Their futures are in our hands. I think a lot of people in the job forget that.'

'I don't,' Caroline replied.

'No, I know. It wasn't a dig at you. And I know I shouldn't, but I carry these sorts of things pretty heavily. They weigh on my mind sometimes. Even little things, like the fact we could be about to ruin Christmas for Kelly. And not just this Christmas, either. Every Christmas after, for years to come, will be a reminder of what happened this year.'

'You can't think like that, Dex.'

'I know, but I do.'

Caroline was silent for a moment. 'You've got a good heart,' she said eventually. 'That's a rare thing, believe me.'

Before Dexter could reply, he was interrupted by the ringing of his mobile phone. He answered it. The voice on the other end of the line was clear and to-the-point.

'Sir, we've had a report of a female threatening to jump from the roof of an industrial building on Lands End Way. We believe the woman is an Antonia Scott — you've got a marker out on her.'

49

'How the bloody hell did she get up there?' Caroline barked, with only Dexter as her audience.

'Christ knows. But it definitely isn't walkable from Aldi. Not in that time. Someone's taken their eye off the ball.'

'Try and get hold of Elijah and Sara,' Caroline said as she swung her Volvo around yet another tight bend. 'They had eyes on. She was in the supermarket, they had sight of her car. There's no way she could have got there in that time unless she's given them the slip. Find out if her car's still there.'

'Will do.'

Caroline took some deep breaths and concentrated on her driving whilst Dexter phoned Sara. It would do her no good to lose her cool now. More than anything, she needed to keep a calm and level head. Even though

Dexter was in charge of the case, she would always ultimately feel the responsibility, and as far as she was concerned it was still her team. More than that, though, a woman's life was now at stake. If Toni Scott jumped to her death, too many people would lose out on answers and closure. She appeared to be the only person who knew everything. Even though Caroline was convinced of her guilt in murdering Clive Thornton, and that would have to be proven, the undeniable fact was that Toni Scott was the missing link. Although identifying and apprehending a killer was always of vital importance, a lot of people missed what that represented. It provided answers. It filled in gaps. It gave closure. And whichever way Caroline looked at it, Toni Scott was the person who held all those cards.

'They hadn't even noticed,' Dexter said, having ended his call.

'What?'

'Toni's car. They hadn't even noticed it'd gone.'

'How the hell can they not notice a car's just disappeared from right under their noses?'

'They got distracted, apparently. A very similar car's now parked in the same space, and they didn't clock it at first.'

Caroline tensed her jaw and tried her hardest not to explode. 'They got distracted? All they had to do was sit in a supermarket car park, one of them watching the door to the supermarket, and the other one watching a car. How on earth do you get distracted from that? Where are we getting these people?'

'We all make mistakes occasionally,' Dexter replied, seeming to be trying to force himself to stay calm, too. 'And you know that's not Sara's style. She doesn't do cock-ups.'

Caroline couldn't argue with his summary, but she could also read the subtext. *There you are. I told you Drummond would mess up eventually.* Although she hadn't been overly keen on Elijah Drummond since he'd arrived, she didn't see any reason to let Dexter's personal vendetta get in the way of proper management.

'That doesn't mean she wasn't bound to make an error at some point,' she said. 'At the very least, they're both responsible. They're sitting in that car right next to each other, with the simplest of jobs. There's no excuse for losing sight of her. I mean, come on. The woman might have jumped to her death by now, for all we know. How the hell is anyone going to explain that to the family? Would you fancy standing up in court at the inquest and telling everyone a woman died and countless people went without justice and answers because you got "distracted"? I hear what you're saying about Sara, Dex, but it just doesn't wash.'

Dexter nodded silently. He clearly still had a lot to learn about managing a team effectively. In any case, when Caroline was in a mood like this, he knew there was nothing to be gained by arguing back with her. Sometimes it was better to just let things lie.

'Yeah,' he replied. 'True. What do you reckon? Another few minutes?'

Caroline instinctively looked down at the centre console of her car, even though the sat nav wasn't on.

'Something like that,' she replied. 'Fingers crossed, Dex. Every second counts.'

50

Caroline's Volvo came to an abrupt halt as she and Dexter took off their seatbelts and got out of the car, heading over towards the industrial unit as hurriedly as they could. They introduced themselves to the uniformed officers at the scene, who guided them up an unlocked external staircase and onto the roof.

In moments like these, a trained negotiator would usually be called, but it was evident they didn't have the luxury of time. In any case, it wasn't the first time Caroline had been in this sort of situation, and her instincts were that she needed to act fast.

'Toni? It's DI Caroline Hills,' she called out. 'We met at your house. My colleague, DS Dexter Antoine is with me. Do you remember? Kelly took a bit of a shine to him.'

The mention of Toni's daughter had been deliberate. The hope was that it would ground her back in reality for long enough to remember she had a daughter who doted on her, and who she'd dedicated her life to.

Caroline hadn't expected Toni to reply, and she'd been right.

'Why don't you step away and come and sit with me?' Caroline called out. 'You're not in any trouble. We just need to make sure everything's okay.'

'It isn't,' Toni replied, just loud enough for Caroline to hear. 'It never will be okay.'

'I know it feels like that now, but it will be. There is a better way through this.'

'All I wanted was justice,' Toni called back. 'If he did what he did to Kelly, then how many others were there? How many would there have been in the future?'

'I can't answer those questions right now, Toni. But I can tell you that a lot of other people would have felt and done the same in your situation.'

'He lied to me. He deceived me. He knew what he was. He knew what he'd done. All he wanted was to preserve his own reputation. His own reality. And you know what? That's where I agree with him. I've always had to fend for myself. I've had no-one. It's just been me, looking after me and everyone else. And I'm not about to stop now.'

'What do you mean, Toni? Can you explain a little more?'

'I'm not going down for this. Not when he got away with what he did for so many years, and never had to spend a day in prison. He should be the one in a cell. Not me. This way, I get to go the same way he did, but at least my conscience will be clear. The same can't be said about him.'

'That's not the right answer, Toni. You can still have a clear conscience without having to take that step. Clive's gone now. He can't harm or hurt anyone anymore. That's the main thing.'

'And why should I listen to you?' Toni barked back. 'You're part of the same crooked system that got us into this mess in the first place. People like him, allowed to roam the streets and harm innocent children, getting away without ever being found guilty of a single thing, and all the while it's someone else who ends up bearing the brunt of it.'

Dexter put a hand on Caroline's shoulder, and called out to Toni.

'Toni? It's DS Dexter Antoine here. Please, think of Kelly. I know you did what you did because you wanted justice for her. I know how much you care about her. I can see that. I saw it at your house when Kelly took a shine to me. She's a lovely girl. She's an absolute credit to you. And she still needs you around. Believe me.'

'She clearly doesn't,' Toni replied. 'She's already shown she's able to fend for herself. She stepped up to the mark. She spoke up for herself. She went to you lot. She's a far stronger person than I gave her credit for, and a far stronger person than me. I always thought she needed me, but I was wrong. It was me who needed her.'

Caroline clenched her jaw involuntarily. She didn't like

the way Toni was talking, putting everything in the past tense. It always struck her how somebody intending to end their own life could go about their normal daily routine right up until that moment. She'd known people leave home in the morning wearing a suit and carrying a briefcase, before throwing themselves in front of a train — having left a suicide note at home half an hour earlier. Toni spending the day at work and then doing the weekly shop wasn't an unusual run of events in the lead up to what Caroline was now witnessing, but it never failed to shock her.

'Of course she needs you,' Dexter replied. 'You need each other.'

Toni shook her head, but didn't look at Dexter. 'She was my crutch. But after finding out what he did... It just changes everything. Everything. I got justice and vengeance for her. That's what matters. That's the important thing. Nothing else matters now. The story's done, and this is how it has to end.'

'Toni, please,' Dexter called back, as he watched her take another step forward. 'What about Run Home?'

Toni appeared to be frozen to the spot. Dexter felt much the same.

'How do you know about that?' Toni said, her voice barely more than a whisper.

'Kelly told me. She said it was her favourite thing in the world.'

For a few moments, Dexter couldn't tell what would happen next. He could see the internal battle Toni was embroiled in, caught between the unshakeable love for her daughter and her determination to end her own life.

'She can play that with anyone,' she eventually replied.

'No. No, she can't. It's you, Toni. It's you she wants.' Dexter could feel the lump rising in his throat, but he knew he couldn't stop now. 'You're the only person who can provide that for her. Truly, I mean. Authentically. You're the only mother she'll ever have. Yes, someone else can play a board game with her, but it's not the board game she loves, is it? It's playing it with her mum. And you're the only mum she'll ever have. She'll never get that feeling anywhere else, no matter how hard she tries to replace it. Once something like that is missing — once it's gone — there's no replicating it. Even if she tries, she'll only ever be comparing it to you. Maybe not consciously, but she will. And it will always come up short. You can replace *a* person, Toni, but you can never replace *the* person.'

It was impossible for Dexter to know whether she'd been truly listening to him and was now processing the words as they began to sink in, or if she'd completely zoned out and was steeling herself for her final jump. Either way, he was out of options. He looked to Caroline.

'Not now, Toni,' Caroline gently called out. 'Let's sit down and get our heads around this properly, shall we? And if you still decide this is what you want to do, no-one can stop you forever. All I'm suggesting is not right now.'

Caroline watched as Toni bowed her head a little, then slowly shook it before turning round.

She waited for Toni to come towards her, and once she was close enough she put her arm around her, giving her crucial human contact and physically ensuring she wouldn't be able to change her mind.

A uniformed police officer approached and guided Toni towards their marked car, informing her that she was under arrest on suspicion of the murder of Clive Thornton.

A few yards away, Caroline watched as Dexter sank slowly onto his haunches and tried to steel himself.

51

The visit to Susan Thornton and her family gave Caroline mixed feelings. It was a crucial part of the process, ensuring the victim's loved ones were updated and helping to provide some element of closure, but she knew it would be some time before the book could finally be closed.

There would be a lengthy and painful court process to come first, in which every detail of Clive's secret life would be disclosed and examined in front of a room full of strangers, in an attempt to determine what had happened and who was responsible. Caroline found this was often the most distressing part for families, and that not only did it drag out the pain of their loss and make it worse, but that it could even taint the happy memories they had of their loved one. Missing a family member who'd been taken from you too soon was one thing, but to discover they'd actually been a monster who'd been living a double life and ruined others? That was the sort of experience that would take a lifetime to even begin to get over.

All of that aside, Caroline still couldn't shake the uneasy feeling that there was something not quite right about Susan Thornton. As was so often the case, it was impossible to put her finger on what it was, but over the years she'd come to trust her intuition and follow it. More often than not, it yielded results.

She and Dexter were sitting in the living room of the Thornton family home, Ross and Emma — Clive and Susan's children — still in temporary residence.

'Emma and I were saying we'll have to stay until after Christmas and New Year,' Ross murmured aside to Caroline as Susan finished making cups of tea in the kitchen. 'She can't be on her own at this time of year. Not this soon. But then after New Year's not much better, is it? They talk about Blue Monday and all of that. Dark winter's nights. It's meant to be the bleakest time of the year for people anyway, without all this going on. But when's the right time? We can't stay forever.'

'It's a tricky one to navigate,' Caroline replied. 'To be honest, I don't think there ever is a right time. Grief's one of those situations where you can easily get it wrong, but there's no real way to get it right. Not one that anyone else can advise on, anyway. Everyone deals with it in different ways. The best thing I could offer you is to suggest you talk about it. Talk about your dad. Talk about what happened. That way you can all process it in your own ways. Just speaking about it and putting it into words can be really therapeutic. It can take the sting out of it, certainly in the long run, even if it makes it more painful right now.'

Ross slowly nodded. 'Yeah, you're right. It's just so difficult to see when you're in the middle of it all. People say "it'll get easier", "please talk to me", "time is a great healer" and all of those things. And deep down you know it's true. They're exactly the things we all say to everyone when they're going through stuff. But it doesn't make a blind bit of difference when you're on the receiving end. You don't want it to heal. You don't want it to get easier. You just want things to go back to the way they were.'

Caroline gave a sympathetic smile. 'I know. But accepting that change has happened is key. That's what moves you out of denial and desperation and into acceptance. It's the only way through. Sorry, I'm aware I'm probably not helping. Like you said, it's the same trite stuff everyone else has been saying.'

'It's okay. I appreciate the sentiment.'

Susan Thornton re-appeared carrying a tray laden with mugs of tea, and put it down on the coffee table before sitting down in an armchair the others had left vacant. As she did so, Ross and Emma exchanged a glance that Caroline and Dexter couldn't quite decode.

'What?' Susan asked, spotting the look. 'It's not as if he's going to be wanting it, is it?'

'Dad's chair,' Ross whispered quietly to Caroline.

'Ah.'

'It's just a chair,' Susan replied. 'It's not like I'm cleaning the toilet rim with his toothbrush.'

'Mum,' Emma said, in a tone that required no further words.

Caroline understood immediately. This was a clear indication that Susan had moved on from denial and desperation, and was now firmly in the oft-visited sub-stage of anger.

'We wanted to come and visit you today to let you know we have someone in custody for Clive's murder,' Caroline said, watching the reactions of each member of his family. Ross seemed professional and unperturbed, Emma shocked and anticipatory. Susan, on the other hand, was a rabbit caught in the headlights. Caroline continued. 'I'm afraid the circumstances of what happened, and what led up to it, might come as a shock. There are some aspects that'll take a while to sink in, and which will likely be quite disturbing to hear. But please know we will support you fully through that process. We have a wonderful team of specially trained officers and support staff who are there to help you.'

'We already know the details of what happened,' Emma said. 'The horseshoe. We got quite a graphic description already. We don't need to hear it again.'

'I wasn't talking about the physical act of murder itself,' Caroline explained. 'It's more the reason why Clive was killed, and events that had led up to his death. Although it won't be easy to hear, it will at least provide an explanation and will help you start to make sense of it all, even if it causes more confusion in the short-term, which I'm sure it will.'

'Just tell us,' Ross said.

Susan remained silent.

Caroline continued. 'The person we've arrested is a woman by the name of Antonia Scott. She often goes by the name Toni. Are you aware of her?'

Emma shook her head. Susan swallowed and blinked.

'A woman?' Ross asked. 'Sorry, I'm aware I'm the only man here, but you're telling me a woman caved my father's head in and killed him?'

'Ross,' Emma said, her voice a pained whisper.

Caroline interjected. 'Yes. We believe it was premeditated. Planned. Your father knew her and trusted her.' Looking at Susan, Caroline could see she'd steeled herself for what was to come next. There was no doubt in her mind that Susan Thornton knew exactly who Toni Scott was. 'I realise this might come as a shock to you, but I'm sorry to say Clive was having an affair with Toni.'

'What? Are you sure?' Emma asked.

'I'm afraid so. I know it might not sound believable, and you'll likely have lots of questions and doubts, but I do need to assure you this is something we hear a lot in our job. These sorts of hidden secrets and aspects of a loved one's life their own families don't know about are remarkably common.'

'So why would she want to kill him?' Ross asked. 'Because he wouldn't leave Mum?'

'We don't think that's the reason, no,' Caroline replied, glancing again at Susan Thornton before she moved on to the next part of her reveal. 'I'm afraid an allegation has been made against your late father. Toni Scott's daughter has alleged that Clive sexually abused her when she was younger.'

Emma brought her hands to her mouth, as if suppressing whatever wanted to come out.

Ross's face dropped. 'What? You must be joking.'

'I'm afraid not, no.'

'How much younger?'

Caroline swallowed and took a breath. 'She claims the incident happened on a camping trip Clive attended whilst she was in the Girl Guides.'

Before Caroline could offer any more information, Emma suddenly rose to her feet and darted out of the room. A couple of seconds later, she heard the sound of the downstairs toilet door being flung open, the plastic toilet seat bashing against the porcelain cistern and Emma vomiting into the bowl.

Caroline gestured to Ross. 'Do you want to…'

'Yeah. Yeah. Course,' he said, standing up and leaving the room to check on his sister.

Caroline looked over at Susan. She was staring at an arbitrary area of carpet on the floor, seemingly lost in another world. It was impossible to guess what she was thinking, and Caroline could only presume her brain had pretty much completely shut down, unable to cope with the enormity of everything that was unfolding.

Now wasn't the time to ambush Susan. Although Caroline was left with no doubt that she'd been well aware of her husband's extra-marital activities, and had gathered from her lack of reaction that she also knew about the allegation against him, there was nothing to be gained by pressing the point right at this moment in time. If nothing else, it would cause enormous anguish to Ross and Emma. In any case, it was crucial they had strong — or at least circumstantial — evidence that Susan knew about the affair and the allegation before Clive's murder. Without evidence, it didn't matter how much the police thought they knew. She could simply deny it, and there was nothing else they could do. The only option was to keep a watchful eye on her, ready to bring her in the moment something else came to light.

As Caroline considered this, her eyes were drawn to a selection of books on the bookcase in the corner of the room. She didn't know how she'd missed them the first time they'd visited, because they stood out like a sore thumb now.

Princess Margaret: A Life Unravelled.

99 Glimpses of Princess Margaret.

Princess Margaret: A Life of Contrasts.

'Who's the one with the interest in the Royal Family?' Caroline asked Susan, who let out a small but noticeable sigh.

'That was Clive. Not the Royal Family as such, but Princess Margaret. He was fascinated by her.'

Before Caroline could ask anything else, Emma and Ross came back into the living room. Emma's face was pale, and Caroline noticed she was shaking slightly.

'Are you okay?' she asked.

Emma merely nodded in response.

'While you're all here, I think it would be helpful to run through the sequence of events that led up to Clive's death, as we understand it. We tend to find this is something that can help provide some closure for families and loved ones, although of course I completely understand if you feel that might be too difficult at the moment.'

Caroline watched as Susan, Ross and Emma looked at one another and exchanged a series of vague shrugs, which she took to mean there was no strong opposition to her suggestion.

'As I was saying, it seems that shortly before his death, Clive was having an affair with Toni Scott. There's some evidence their relationship had been coming to an end recently, but we're yet to establish the full circumstances of that. We believe Toni's daughter, on seeing Clive dropping Toni back home one night, recognised him and suffered a series of traumatic memories. I won't go into the details today. Following that, she confided in her mum and told her what had happened to her all those years ago. It seems Toni ultimately believed her daughter, but that this happened gradually over a course of time. We don't know at which point Toni decided she had to take the law into her own hands, but we do know that she believed the police wouldn't take her daughter seriously, and that the only way justice — as she saw it — could be obtained would be for her to dispense it herself. In my experience, for what it's worth, I can say it would have been extremely difficult to have compiled a case against Clive based purely on her testimony alone.'

'But surely that's a good thing,' Ross said. 'What if he didn't do it?'

'He did it,' Emma replied, without looking at him. 'There's no point trying to defend it now.'

Caroline continued, if only to head this debate off at the pass. 'It seems Toni's plans to end your father's life were premeditated. There would have been a fair amount of planning involved. Her method of entering Oakham Castle meant she wasn't picked up on CCTV, and we don't believe that's a coincidence. The castle and its grounds are pretty well covered by the cameras, but she managed to pick a route that took advantage of various blind spots. This also gave her the advantage of being able to cut the power to the building once she was inside, making sure she wouldn't be picked up on the internal cameras. Once she'd done that, it was fairly straightforward for her to approach Clive, who wouldn't have seen her as a threat at that point.'

Caroline stopped for a moment, realising she was going to have to include an amount of rather awkward background at this point.

'Toni and your father's relationship was quite different and unconventional. Once Toni was inside the Great Hall of the castle, she persuaded Clive to sit in the judge's chair while she tied him to it, apparently as part of a game or sexual act. At that point, she took one of the horseshoes down from the wall and used it to kill him.'

Ross let out a long exhalation. 'Jesus Christ,' he said eventually.

Caroline sympathised. 'I know it's a lot to take in. A lot to get your head around. It's difficult enough coming to terms with the death of a loved one as it is, without all of the other revelations on top of that. I can't even begin to imagine what you're going through.'

'If I'm completely honest, I'm not sure I can either,' Ross replied. 'It feels like you're talking about another person. It doesn't seem real.'

'Things will sink in slowly over time. Don't worry about trying to make sense of it all now. It won't.'

'That'll come gradually,' Dexter added. 'For now, we just wanted to make sure you had all the information as we understand it, so you're not left wondering. You wouldn't want to be left with unanswered questions. That's the real killer.'

Caroline instinctively closed her eyes and sighed inwardly.

Dexter, meanwhile, flapped. 'I mean…'

'It's okay. We know what you mean,' Emma said, a wry smile appearing at the corners of her mouth. 'If you can't find dark humour even in the worst situations, what's the point?'

52

Back at the office later that day, Caroline was still ruminating over her concerns about Susan Thornton. How much did she know, and when did she know it? And crucially, what did this mean for the case?

'Don't think too hard,' Dexter said as he sauntered past. 'You might pop an eyeball.'

Caroline smiled with one corner of her mouth, not fully removed from her thoughts. He so often seemed able to read her mind. It would have been useful, she thought, if he was able to do the next bit and piece all of her thoughts together so she could just be presented with the final summary, but — as was always the case — that was up to her.

'Seriously,' he continued, 'it'll all come out in the wash. There's no point wasting your energy on it now. You've got a family waiting at home for you.'

Caroline thought of Mark and the boys, and the journey they'd all been on over the past couple of years.

'Yeah. You're right,' she said. 'As per usual.'

Dexter smiled at her, then walked back to his desk.

Reaching over to shut down her computer, Caroline noticed an email pinging into her inbox. The subject line immediately caught her attention. She glanced at the clock. Surely she could spare a minute or two? She opened the email and read its contents carefully.

It was a report from the team that'd searched Toni Scott's house and removed anything that might have been of evidential interest. Nestled among the list of items was something that jumped out.

Multipick Quick-Key molding and key duplication kit.

In that moment, everything started to piece together in her mind.

53

Dexter allowed himself the briefest moment of joy as he remembered tomorrow would be his last day at work before his Christmas break. He didn't have any major plans for the festive season, and he knew he'd have to make sure his days were filled with plans. For him, keeping busy was often crucial.

He'd popped into Oakham on his lunch break earlier that day, and had found exactly what he was looking for. Now, as he made a small diversion to his route home and pulled up a few doors down from the address in Twyford, he was looking forward to spreading a little bit of his own Christmas cheer.

He didn't know how Kelly Scott would be coping now she was living here with her aunt, rather than the familiar surroundings she knew from being at home with her mother. He'd wondered if he might be able to help her regain some familiarity at the same time as embracing new beginnings, and he smiled to himself as he reached over to the passenger seat and picked up the wrapped board game he'd bought earlier. Ludo — the same game Kelly knew as Run Home — familiar, but still fresh.

It was hard to predict how she might react, but Dexter was hopeful. In any case, he told himself he had something of an advantage. Kelly liked him and trusted him. He wasn't sure why, and had no idea what he'd done that no-one else had, but even on a purely professional level it was always a huge advantage when victims and witnesses felt they liked and trusted the police. No-one ever gave helpful information to someone they didn't like or trust.

He switched off his car engine, feeling the warm air rescinding as the heaters wound down and the icy December chill started to worm its way in almost immediately. He was about to reach for the door handle and step out when he saw movement at Kelly's aunt's house.

He watched as Susan Thornton stepped out into the driveway, gave a wave towards the house, then got into her car, started the engine and pulled away.

54

Eventually, Dexter realised he'd had two options. He could have followed Susan and spoken to her to find out why she'd been visiting her husband's victim, or he could have gone to Kelly's aunt's house as planned and asked them what Susan had been doing there a few moments earlier.

As it happened, he'd done neither. He'd simply frozen in that moment, a complete crisis of confidence paralysing him into indecision. It wasn't a feeling he was familiar with, and it worried him.

It was now too late to follow Susan Thornton, and he'd got himself into such a state he felt there was no way he could visit Kelly and put on the cheerful, jovial act he'd need to. Instead, he gave himself a few minutes to compose himself, then he called Caroline and told her what had happened.

'Did you follow her?' she asked, hammering home his own feelings of regret and stupidity.

'I tried, but she caught me off guard and was heading in the opposite direction. There was nowhere to turn, and by that point she was long gone,' he lied.

'Damn. Did she see you?'

'No, I don't think so.'

'Then she was probably heading home. Good job on following your gut, though. You're right — something seems really odd about this. I'll get someone to head over and keep an eye on her house, so we can see if she goes straight back.'

55

The next morning, Caroline and Dexter sat down in the interview room opposite Toni Scott and her solicitor.

'Okay, Toni. This is our second interview following your arrest on suspicion of the murder of Clive Thornton. When we spoke in the first interview, we were mostly trying to ascertain what had gone on, and to determine the circumstances surrounding Clive's death. You weren't particularly forthcoming. I don't know if that was concern for your daughter, or the advice of your solicitor, but we really do need to get to the bottom of things now. For everyone's sake, including Kelly's.'

'How's she doing?' Toni asked.

'She's fine. She's with your sister. She's going to be looking after Kelly now.'

Toni nodded solemnly. She clearly knew it could be some time before she saw her daughter again, and she certainly wasn't likely to be out of prison for some years. A smart barrister would be able to minimise the sentence by highlighting the abuse Kelly had been subjected to and the horrors that Clive had inflicted, but there was no way around the fact that Toni had planned to and succeeded in murdering him. Although many people would have happily let her walk free under the circumstances, a crime had clearly been committed, and an-eye-for-an-eye wasn't a defence in law.

'Can I ask you an odd question, Toni? Did Clive have an interest in the Royal Family at all?'

Toni smiled slightly, as if Caroline had asked her if Eskimos like the cold.

'He had an interest in Princess Margaret. An obsession, I'd have called it. Clive was a couple of years too young to have made the most of the swinging sixties, but the whole hedonistic vibe was something that fascinated him. He loved the hidden side of society. He was totally... What's the word — captivated — by Princess Margaret's reputation as a good time girl. The idea that she could be the Queen's sister — a senior member of the Royal Family — and at the same time be living this completely self-indulgent and carefree lifestyle completely mesmerised him.'

'Which is why you chose that horseshoe, correct?'

Toni didn't reply. Caroline continued.

'It was poetic justice, wasn't it? Like Princess Margaret, Clive had lived his public life very differently to how he did in private. He'd had to reconcile those two parts of himself. And ultimately, although in very different ways, they both met untimely ends due to their private excesses. I mean, I don't know if you put quite that much thought into it, but I imagine on seeing the horseshoes available to you there was only ever going to be one choice.

'Listen,' Caroline said, leaning forward and resting her elbows on the table. 'When we searched your house, we found something quite interesting.' She took out a photo of the key copying kit and pushed it across the table to her. 'Can you tell me what this is?'

Toni looked at the photo, her face passive but the length of her gaze telling Caroline all she needed to know.

'It's a key copying kit,' Caroline said. 'You use it to make impressions of keys in clay moulds, which you can then cast new keys with. It's a clever little way of copying them. What did you need this for, Toni?'

The solicitor put his hand on the table. 'Is there anything to suggest that this item was actually purchased or owned by Ms Scott?' he asked, the question dripping with subtext.

'It was in her house, amongst her belongings. So yes, I'd say there's quite a lot that suggests that. Can you tell me what you needed it for, Toni?'

Toni Scott remained quiet.

Caroline decided to launch another curveball. 'Do you recognise this item?' she asked, passing across a photograph of a horseshoe. 'We discovered it buried in one of the flowerbeds in your garden. Can you tell me how it got there?'

Toni's eyes stayed locked onto the photo, but she didn't respond.

'I don't think Ms Scott will be making any comment at this time,' the solicitor said.

Caroline ignored him. 'Okay, well if you don't want to tell us, the only option we've got is to put our own theories out there and see how they land. So how about I tell you what I think happened? I think you broke into Clive Thornton's house that night. I don't think it was a burglar who got interrupted before they managed to get anything. I think it was you, and you got exactly what you were after. You wanted to copy his keys — specifically his key to Oakham Castle. That's how you managed to get into the castle through the back door, and how you managed to hide yourself away without being spotted on CCTV or coming in through the main entrance. You knew you could tell Clive you'd come in the usual way and he just hadn't seen you. Maybe it was all part of one of your roleplaying games. I don't know. But I think that's how you got in. We know you didn't use the main entrance, and we know you weren't picked up on CCTV. Then all you had to do was wait for Clive to close the castle for the night, cut the power so you wouldn't be picked up on the internal CCTV, and then you were free to come out and do what you did.'

'Do you have anything other than wild theory, Detective Inspector?' the solicitor asked.

Caroline ignored him again. 'You see, this all seems to make perfect sense to me so far, Toni. But there was something that didn't quite seem to fit. Again, it was the break-in at Clive and Susan Thornton's place. We know the person who broke in didn't take anything, and the theory was they'd been disturbed and disappeared before they'd taken anything. Strange they got away with absolutely nothing, but not unheard of. But what didn't quite fit was that Clive reported the break-in to the police the next morning, and when the police called back, Susan answered the phone and was clear that they didn't want to pursue the matter further. Of course, I understand that nothing was taken and maybe they thought there was no need for any action, but if your house has just been broken into, you feel scared. Unsafe. Insecure. You want the police to catch whoever did it, if only to make sure they won't come back and try again. You don't just replace the broken window and carry on as if nothing ever happened. Unless, of course, you knew the person who'd broken it, or if you'd somehow managed to mete out your own form of justice.'

'What are you insinuating, DI Hills?' the solicitor asked.

Caroline watched as tears began to form in Toni's eyes.

'She didn't do anything wrong,' Toni said, eventually. 'She stood by that man for years. She shut herself off to all his ways, all the things he'd tried to keep hidden behind closed doors. She kept herself just the other side of the door, standing guard over it, never quite knowing what was behind it either. And do you know why? Because she didn't want to look inside. She couldn't bear to think about what she might find. She kept herself firmly swept up in the narrative he'd woven for everyone else, too. And why wouldn't she? If she did otherwise, it meant her whole adult life had been a lie.'

'What happened, Toni?'

Toni looked away and shook her head as more tears began to fall.

'What'll happen to Susan?'

'That depends entirely on what she's done.'

'Nothing. She did nothing. That's my whole point.'

In that moment, Caroline was pretty sure she knew exactly what Toni meant.

'When you say she did nothing…'

Toni sighed and leaned back in her chair. 'I mean she did nothing.'

'Did you know Susan went to visit Kelly at your sister's house?'

Caroline watched as Toni registered this — the reaction on her face unmissable.

'When?'

'Last night. You might as well tell us what happened, Toni. What was Susan's involvement in this? Did she put you up to it?'

'No. Like I said, she did nothing.'

'But she knew what you were going to do?'

Toni's silence told Caroline all she needed to know. Caroline leaned forward on her elbows again.

'Toni, I think everyone's had enough of lies and deceit for one lifetime, don't you? This whole sorry saga was all to do with the truth coming out once and for all. It's not going to do anyone any favours to hide things at this stage.'

'I know. But I don't want to see another wronged woman going down and being punished for what that man did.'

'This has nothing to do with what Clive Thornton did, Toni. It's to do with what Susan Thornton did or didn't do. That's all we're interested in at this moment in time. When you broke into the house, did Susan apprehend you?'

Toni gave a slight, almost imperceptible nod. 'She had the fright of her life. She heard a noise and thought the cat had knocked something over. I think the only reason she didn't start screaming was because she could see I was as scared as she was.'

'And did you talk?'

Toni nodded again. 'It all came out. It couldn't not. We sat and talked for over an hour. Clive was out cold. He's been on sleeping tablets for years. It all adds up now. Who on earth could fall asleep easily with all that on his conscience? So I told her everything. I told her about our affair. I told her what he'd done to Kelly. And I told her I'd broken in to make a copy of his keys, so I could make sure he got what he deserved.'

'Did you tell her you were planning to murder him?'

Toni shook her head. 'No. She didn't ask, and I didn't tell.'

Caroline registered the meaning of this. Without clear

evidence, claiming conspiracy to murder would be difficult, to say the least. But she had no doubt in her mind that Susan Thornton must have at least considered the possibility that this was what Toni had been insinuating. In any case, at the very least, she'd simply sat back and let events take their course.

'So what, she just said "Sure, take the keys and do what you like"?' Caroline asked.

'Not quite, no. Nothing was really said. She just stood up and went to go back upstairs.'

'And did she?'

'She was about to. But then I asked her to do something for me.'

'Go on.'

'I asked her to keep an eye on Kelly. Check in on her. If I ended up going anywhere. I didn't say prison. I don't know if I was even thinking prison. In my mind, I was probably thinking of a wooden box. But I asked her to watch over her from time to time. If she could.'

'And what did she say?'

'She didn't say anything.'

Caroline watched as Toni looked down at her own hands. To her, this was a tale of two women, each remarkable in their own way, dealing with extreme trauma in two very different fashions. And it struck her that Susan Thornton, a woman who rarely said a word, could still so often say so much.

56

Caroline sat down in Chief Superintendent Derek Arnold's office, having been called in to see him "at her earliest convenience". She had an idea as to how it might go: he'd congratulate her, point out the levels of funding and resources were clearly proven adequate, mention a couple of things she could've done better, then wish her all the best and send her on her way.

The meeting started with Arnold steepling his hands in front of his face as he observed her, like she was some sort of exhibit in a zoo.

'Not the outcome any of us expected a few days ago, is it?' he said.

'Well, no,' Caroline replied. 'But with all due respect, sir, if we'd known everything a few days ago, we wouldn't be sitting here now.'

'I was referring more to the use of police resources in flying over to Norway to chase a dead end lead.'

Caroline bit her tongue. It had been Arnold's suggestion to go to Norway — not hers — but she knew it wouldn't get her anywhere to point that out. 'Bearing in mind the information we had available to us at the time, and the position we were in, I still believe that was the right decision. Of course, had we known what we know now, we would have done things differently. But we didn't. So we couldn't.'

Arnold nodded slowly. 'I see what you're saying. But that doesn't mean everyone in the food chain sees it that way. And the problem with food chains is that it's the next creature down the line that gets eaten alive. If they didn't, we'd have lions and tigers running around eating wheat and maize. I've got to report up the line, just the same as you. It's easy for me to justify that sort of frivolity if it leads to a result, but I'm going to have my pants pulled down big time over this.'

Caroline wanted to ask him why he felt that was her problem, but she thought better of it. 'If it helps, sir, I think it can certainly be justified as leading to a result. By effectively eliminating our main suspect, it allowed us to focus our energies elsewhere, which ultimately did lead us to identifying and apprehending the killer.'

'Yes. About that,' Arnold replied. 'This would be the killer you had under tight surveillance, but who managed to escape that surveillance — and almost escape justice — despite being watched over by your officers.'

Caroline pursed her lips. 'Yes, we have identified some procedural issues which could do with tightening up,' she replied. 'But again, ultimately that minor slip-up didn't lead to catastrophe, and we were able to get a result.'

'It might not have led to catastrophe, but it certainly isn't something to be proud of,' Arnold replied. 'It triggered a panic response, it led to members of the public being disturbed by seeing a woman about to jump to her death, and more than anything it highlighted a complete lack of professionalism on the part of your officers. What more basic elements of policing are there than just sitting in a car and watching a building?'

Caroline didn't have an answer to this. As unreasonable as it felt, she knew Arnold was right. She just didn't see the point in him hammering it home. It wasn't as if she didn't know what had gone wrong or wouldn't be putting measures in place to make sure nothing of the sort ever happened again.

Arnold continued. 'If I were you, I'd be looking for answers. Because my governors will be. And I can only get those answers from you. Don't make me look like a tit at the top table, Caroline. We might be lucky. We might not. But sooner or later, if things continue like this, they're going to be asking for heads. And it bloody well won't be mine that rolls, I can tell you that. Jesus, what a story for DS Drummond to tell to his pals in EMSOU.'

The subtle meaning behind Arnold's comment wasn't lost on Caroline.

'I still believe that ultimately the result speaks for itself, sir. By hook or by crook, we identified the killer, apprehended her and ensured no further damage was done to people or property. Yes, it may have been resource-heavy. And yes, we could have apprehended Toni Scott a few minutes earlier. But we didn't, and yet we still achieved the same result.'

Arnold stayed silent for a while. 'The truth is, we'll never really know, will we?' he said eventually and unhelpfully.

'Quite, sir,' Caroline replied.

'Well. Fingers crossed, eh?'

Caroline gave a single nod. 'Fingers crossed, sir.'

57

The familiar Christmas pop songs were a welcome sound for Caroline, as she sat down at a table in The Wheatsheaf in Oakham alongside Dexter, Aidan, Sara and Elijah. She wasn't usually keen on hearing the same dozen tracks every December, but this year she'd decided she was going to throw herself fully into the Christmas spirit. After all, it'd provide the distraction and relief she needed after a busy and turbulent year.

It'd become something of a tradition to pull the whole team together for some celebratory drinks after the closure of a case, but tonight wouldn't be a late one for her — she had somewhere else to be.

For the others, the drinks were already in full flow, and Christmas cheer was certainly in abundance. Elijah, though, seemed a little distracted by his phone, and was firing off text messages to somebody at a rate of knots.

Before Caroline could ask if everything was okay, he excused himself and headed outside to make a phone call.

Seconds later, a new song came on and Aidan and Sara both gave a triumphant cheer of recognition, before leaping to their feet and finding a space near the bar they'd now designated as their dance floor.

'Looks like they're having fun,' Caroline said to Dexter, who was now the only other person at the table.

'Got to let your hair down every now and again,' Dexter replied.

'You not tempted to get up and join them?'

'Can't say I am.'

'You still planning to spend tomorrow with your parents?' Caroline asked, noticing the slight flicker of emotion cross his face as he heard her words.

'Yeah, hopefully. Just organising times and stuff,' he replied. Caroline wasn't fully convinced by his answer.

'You have got plans, haven't you?' she asked.

'Yeah, just got to sort details, I think.'

'You think? It's Christmas Eve, Dex.'

'Yeah, I know. They don't live far away, though. It's just been a bit tricky recently.'

'Between you and them?'

'Between me and everything.'

Caroline could see a look on his face that told her all wasn't well.

'Dex, talk to me,' she said. 'What's the matter?'

'I'm alright,' he replied. 'Just been letting things get on

top of me a bit too much recently, that's all. Nothing to worry about.'

'You're forgetting I'm a copper too, Dex. I know when someone's not telling me the truth, or hiding something. You're not okay, are you?'

'I am,' Dexter replied.

She realised there was no point pushing the subject too hard, and resolved herself to checking in on him more regularly. He'd talk when he was ready.

Unnoticed by Caroline, Dexter tensed his jaw and closed his eyes.

'Actually, boss,' he said, 'there is something I need to tell you.'

Before either of them could say another word, the door of the pub clattered open and Elijah came back in, sitting himself back down at the table.

'Alright?' he asked, clearly having noticed the uneasy atmosphere.

'Fine,' Caroline replied. 'You?'

'Yeah. Just family stuff,' Elijah replied, before looking up towards the bar and the makeshift dance floor Sara and Aidan had formed.

Although he'd tried to suppress it, Caroline recognised the look of jealousy and surprise on Elijah's face. It was one she'd seen before.

'Looks like they share a favourite Christmas song,' she said.

'Looks like it. Anyone for another drink?'

'I'm alright, thanks,' Caroline said, looking at the series of full glasses they each still had.

Regardless, Elijah stood up and headed for the bar, stopping en route to ask Sara if she wanted another drink, but neglecting to ask Aidan. A few moments later, he returned with one pint of lager, and sat down in the middle chair of three on the other side of the table. Caroline immediately recognised it as an attempt to make sure Sara and Aidan wouldn't be able to sit next to each other when they came back. There had been a couple of things at work that had made her wonder, but by now she was pretty certain that Elijah was keen on Sara at the very least. If she'd been a betting woman, she would have put money on them already being in a relationship but having kept it hidden from everyone else.

Sure enough, as the song finished, the pair returned and each took a seat either side of Elijah, having been left with no other options.

'Having fun?' Elijah said to Sara.

'God, yes. It feels so good to kick back and relax. You not coming up for a dance?'

'Maybe later,' Elijah replied.

He gave a slight eye roll as his phone began to ring again. Glancing briefly at the screen, he made a brief apology to the others, then headed out towards the garden to take the call.

'Is he okay?' Sara asked Caroline and Dexter.

'He's fine,' Caroline replied. 'Just trying to sort out Christmas arrangements, I think.'

'Oh? I thought he was— I mean, I presumed he would have already sorted that out by now.'

'Not everyone's as organised as you, Sara, more's the pity,' Caroline said, pushing her chair back and standing up. 'Back in a mo. Just heading to the little girls' room.'

Caroline walked towards the back of the pub and out into the corridor that led to the toilets. As she got there, she saw Elijah standing outside, next to the door, his back towards her. Despite the glass between them, she could hear every word.

'We can still go to your mum's,' he was saying, his voice tight and frustrated. 'It'll just have to be a bit later than usual, that's all. Yeah, I know. I can't help that. It's a new job, I can't just suddenly tell them I'm not going to do it. Yeah. Yeah, I know. Listen, it'll only be a couple of hours, I promise. I'll be back by late morning. Alright, we'll speak about it later. Love you too.'

58

The comforting smell of mulled wine hit Caroline full in the face as she opened the front door of her house, closely followed by the sounds of an indeterminate Christmas film the kids were watching on the telly.

'Ah, there she is,' Mark said as he came out of the kitchen wiping his hands on a tea towel. 'That Santa all banged up in a cell for a few days, then?'

'Don't let them hear you say that,' Caroline replied, smiling and gesturing towards the living room. 'Are you making mulled wine?'

'My own recipe,' Mark said, beaming. 'Well, Jamie Oliver's, but I tweaked it so I'm calling it mine.'

'Smells lovely. Although I was going to suggest maybe getting a last-minute babysitter and seeing if we could try and catch that film at the cinema again.'

'So you can actually see the whole thing this time?' Mark asked, with humour.

'No, so I can apologise and make it up to you.'

'I tell you what,' he said, moving towards her and putting his arms round her waist. 'Why don't you think of some other way to make it up to me?'

Caroline put her arms on his shoulders. 'One thing I can tell you is I'm pretty sure you've been over-testing that mulled wine already.'

'See? Not safe to drive. We'll have to stay in.'

'Smart. We can't leave the kids on Christmas Eve, anyway. How about we go between Christmas and New Year?'

'Perfect. We can make use of one of those days where nobody knows what actual day of the week it is, and only refer to them by the number.'

Caroline smiled. 'I like your thinking. But I do have another little surprise for you, and I hope you won't be too inebriated to take me up on this one.'

'Oh?'

'I popped into the travel agents in town earlier and booked us a little break. February half term. A week away with the boys.'

'Are you serious?' Mark replied, a warm smile appearing across his face.

'Yup. And a bit warmer than Suffolk this time. We're off to Cyprus!'

Mark hugged Caroline and held her tight. 'Caz, that's amazing. Are you sure you're okay with the time off?'

'Yep. And I've already told them not to bother phoning

me about anything. Dex will be the on-call SIO, whether he likes it or not. I'll turn my phone off if I have to.'

Mark raised an eyebrow. 'And you had the audacity to suggest I'd been drinking.'

'What say you to pouring us a couple of large mugs of that mulled wine, grabbing the Christmas biscuits and falling asleep under the blanket with the kids?'

'As long as you're tucked up in bed before midnight,' Mark said, wagging his finger. 'Wouldn't want you missing out on a visit from Santa, would we? Assuming one of your colleagues lets him out the clink in time.'

Caroline smiled. 'Wouldn't dream of it.'

WANT MORE?

I hope you enjoyed *Moment of Truth*.

If you want to be the first to hear about new books — and get a couple of free short stories in the meantime — head to:

adamcroft.net/vip-club

Two free short stories will be sent to you straight away, and you'll be the first to hear about new releases.

For more information, visit my website: **adamcroft.net**

ACKNOWLEDGEMENTS

I don't think I've ever found a book easy to write, despite what the end product might indicate. Sometimes a writer can be derailed by their own plot, or external factors in life could get in the way. In writing *Moment of Truth*, I had the 'pleasure' of experiencing both on a scale and magnitude I never had before.

To say this past year has been the most stressful, draining and intense period of my life would be an understatement. Writing has been, at different stages, both a cathartic experience and a huge pressure. It's provided a welcome distraction and release from the exhaustion of real life when I needed it most, but I've been acutely aware that my brain needed to be fully engaged to make sure I gave you the best book possible.

This book nearly didn't get started. Then it nearly didn't get finished. But it did. And although I'll happily splash my name over the cover and take the credit (and money), this book simply wouldn't exist without the practical and moral support of many wonderful people.

For their feedback on an early draft of the book, my thanks go to Lucy, Bev, Manuela, Jim, Karina and Mark. Mark also needs extra thanks for helping me untangle myself after I'd managed to get the plot wrapped round my neck with one leg in the air.

To Nick Castle, for designing another cracking cover.

To Graham Bartlett, former Chief Superintendent and City Commander of Brighton & Hove Police, for all his help and advice on police procedure.

To Ant, for being an absolute rock and the best friend anyone could ask for.

To Lisa, Mark, Emma, Adam, Simon, Stan, Gemma and everyone else who's been there in their own way over the past year, no matter how small or insignificant they thought their contribution to be. Speaking from this end, each of them was a huge help.

But I genuinely wouldn't have written this book if it wasn't for you, the reader. My biggest thanks go to you.

A SPECIAL THANK YOU TO MY MEMBERS

Thank you to everyone who's a member of my VIP Premium readers club. Active supporters get a number of benefits, including the chance of having a character named after them in my books. In this book, PC Ian Harding, Clare Garner and Alyson Marlor were named after subscribers.

With that, I'd like to give my biggest thanks to my small but growing group of Patreon supporters: Adrian Smith, Aimee Braiden, Alan Betts, Alexier Mayes, Alyson Marlor, Amanda Boakes, Andrew Jeens, Angela Edwards, Angela Kane, Angela Pepper, Ann Hall, Ann Sidey, Bethan Brown, Brian Savory, Carole Beeton, Cheryl Hill, Chris and Sue, Chris Armitage, Christine Hoskin, Claire Evans, Clare Garner, Damon Cannon, Dawn Broughton, Dawn Godsall, Dee Fox, Estelle Golding, Esther Cross, Estie Sage, George Fitzpatrick, Gordon Aldred, Hayley McDonnell, Helen Brown, Hilary Blackmore, Ian Harding, Jeanette Moss, Jeanie Vickers, Jeremy Thompson, Julie Benson, Julie Cornelius, Karina Gallagher, Kathleen Burley, Keith Neale, Ken Hassan, Kenneth Mounser, Kerry Robb, Kevin Winfield, Kirstin Wallace, Leonard Burke, Lesley Somerville, Linda

Anderson, Lisa Bayliss, Lisa-marie Thompson, Lynne Lester-George, Mary Fortey, Maureen Ansell, Maureen Hutchings, Mike Greenaway, Nigel Gibbs, Pam Donnelly, Peter Tottman, Paul Wardle, Peter Walmsley, Phillip Zirkle, Rachel Royle, Ray Short, Richard Berrett, Richard Sheehan, Rodney Turner, Ruby Whitfield, Russell Mitchell, Russell Nelson, Sally Catling, Sally Chapman, Sally Tagg, Sally-Anne Coton, Sarah Sims, Sean Halliday, Sharon Louth, Sharon Oakes, Shelly Jones, Stephen Vitali, Susan Fiddes, Susan Stone, Teresa Goodbun, Tremayne Alflatt, Tricia Naylor Budd, Wanda Frye, and Wendy. You're all absolute superstars.

If you're interested in becoming a member, please head over to **adamcroft.net/membership**. Your support is hugely appreciated.

EXCLUSIVE MEMBERSHIP BENEFITS

Are you an avid reader of my books? If so, you can gain access to exclusive members-only books, content and more.

By subscribing to VIP Premium, you'll get a whole host of benefits and additional perks — and supporting me and my work directly.

Here are just a few of the benefits you can enjoy:

- **Up to 30% off** all online shop orders from adamcroft.net
- **Early access to new books** — up to *2 weeks* before release
- A **free ebook** of your choice
- **Free short stories**, not available anywhere else
- Have a **character named after you** in future books

- Access to **exclusive** videos and behind-the-scenes content
- A **personalised video message** from me
- Unlimited **free UK postage** (and reduced international shipping)
- **Your name in the Acknowledgements** of every new book
- Access to **exclusive** blog posts

To find out more, or to join today, head to **adamcroft. net/membership.**

HAVE YOU LISTENED TO THE RUTLAND AUDIOBOOKS?

The Rutland crime series is now available in audiobook format, narrated by Leicester-born **Andy Nyman** (Peaky Blinders, Unforgotten, Star Wars) and **Mathew Horne** (Gavin & Stacey, The Catherine Tate Show, Horne & Corden).

The series is available from all good audiobook retailers and libraries now, published by W.F. Howes on their QUEST and Clipper imprints.

W.F. Howes are one of the world's largest audiobook publishers and have been based in Leicestershire since their inception.

ADAM CROFT

With over two million books sold to date, Adam Croft is one of the most successful independently published authors in the world, having sold books in over 120 different countries.

In February 2017, Amazon's overall Author Rankings briefly placed Adam as the most widely read author in the world at that moment in time, with J.K. Rowling in second place. And he still bangs on about it.

Adam is considered to be one of the world's leading experts on independent publishing and has been featured on BBC television, *BBC Radio 4*, *BBC Radio 5 Live*, the *BBC World Service*, *The Guardian*, *The Huffington Post*, *The Bookseller* and a number of other news and media outlets.

In March 2018, Adam was conferred as an Honorary Doctor of Arts, the highest academic qualification in the UK, by the University of Bedfordshire in recognition of his services to literature.

Adam presents the regular crime fiction podcast *Partners in Crime* with fellow bestselling author and television actor Robert Daws.